He gave Lucy an intimate look

"You would make a perfect Cinderella," he murmured, "with your hair loose."

"Would I?" Lucy asked nervously.

He set his glass down and reached to pull out one of the pins. And another, and another. Lucy sat there, unmoving, until every hairpin was gone and her long blond hair fell in disheveled waves around her shoulders.

"That's better," Laurent said critically. He combed his fingers slowly through the tresses.

"I thought you'd like it done up," she said.

He shook his head. "Next time, leave it like that."

Next time? But there wouldn't be a next time, Lucy thought. How could there be, when he was so full of secrets, so...dishonest?

English author **SALLY COOK** lives in Norwich with her two small sons. She has been a professional writer for nine years, but only recently has branched into fiction.

Books by Sally Cook

HARLEQUIN ROMANCE
41—TAKEOVER BID

SALLY COOK

deep harbour

Harlequin Books

TORONTO • NEW YORK • LONDON
AMSTERDAM • PARIS • SYDNEY • HAMBURG
STOCKHOLM • ATHENS • TOKYO • MILAN

Harlequin Presents first edition December 1989
ISBN 0-373-11223-8

Original hardcover edition published in 1988
by Mills & Boon Limited

CHAPTER ONE

AUGUST. A hot day, very hot. The kind of day when all the tourists thought of boat rides, and every ticket was sold well before midday. Lucy had unrolled the awning on the *San Felipe* so that most of the wooden benches were in the shade.

A small boy, perhaps six or seven, rushed right to the bows and crawled across the white-painted boarding that filled in the sharp end of the boat. His mother followed more slowly and sat on one of the benches, and Lucy thought of warning the woman to call the boy back to sit next to her. The tourists didn't realise how deep Mahon harbour was, they seemed to think it was perfectly safe because the water was so still.

The *San Felipe* was a little boat. Juan squeezed on as many tourists as possible on busy days, but it didn't do to squash them too much when they were paying four hundred pesetas each. There were thirty-five paying customers that afternoon: a full boat-load, plus Juan and herself. She had sized each one up as they boarded. No Germans, two elderly French ladies, in chic black frocks, and the usual succession of English: young couples from the cheaper hotels, families with children from the apartments, and middle-aged couples from the posh hotel on the clifftop.

She checked that all the passengers were settled, then nodded to Juan and jumped back onshore. Juan pulled in the gangplank and Lucy unfastened the mooring rope. Then Juan reached out a callused hand to help her back on board, and they were off.

Soon they were out of the narrow bay of Cala Corb where the *San Felipe* was moored, and chugging down the south-western side of the main harbour inlet. All the shoreline was densely inhabited. Bays, restaurants, historic houses, boats large and small, followed each other in dense profusion. Quiet, sleepy Villa Carlos gave way to bustling Mahon town, with its yacht club, with its commercial wharfs where great cargo vessels tied up and the car ferries disgorged their passengers from Palma and Barcelona, and with its naval station.

Juan hugged the coastline closely along this side, though the harbour was fairly narrow everywhere, and they were never more than half a mile from either shore. Then he brought the *San Felipe* across the blunt nose of the harbour, and down the north-eastern side.

The naval installations of Mahon came first: the grey ships of the Spanish navy, and the white buildings that dated from the time when the English navy had moored in the same locations. Then the shore grew quieter. There were no towns on the north-eastern shore of the harbour, no villages even. Just a succession of villas, perched on the steep shoreline.

Juan kept a little farther from the shore here, since many yachts were anchored in the still water, and several of the sheltered inlets were roped off to protect delicate clam beds. The tourists gazed indifferently at the imposing villas. Lucy thought this the least interesting stretch of the boat trip. She knew some of the other boat guides recited the names of the more illustrious residents to liven it up. But she never copied them: it seemed to her like an intrusion, and though all the people who lived here were rich, few were internationally famous enough for their names to be known to the tourists. Instead she began to talk about the history of Minorca, and the days when the English had controlled the island.

The harbour was quiet as the *San Felipe* made her way downstream. The big ferries were still loading at the docks; the fishermen were enjoying their siestas. Only a few yachts and motorboats zigzagged across the broad channel. Then a power-boat pulled off suddenly from the shore, about fifty yards ahead of the *San Felipe*.

The noise drowned Lucy's steady commentary for a moment, and she saw Juan's lips move in a colourful Catalan curse as the wash from the power-boat rolled towards the *San Felipe*. Its bows lifted in the water, and it rolled and tipped as the waves passed under it.

'Sorry about that, ladies and gentlemen,' Lucy said cheerfully. 'Just a taster of what it'll feel like when we round the end of the harbour.' A few of the younger English tourists smiled politely, and the elderly Frenchwomen stared balefully until Lucy began to translate this into French.

She hadn't reached the end of her French sentence when the power-boat, arcing round in midstream, came hurtling back towards the *San Felipe*. This time it cut much closer, less than ten yards from the *San Felipe*'s bows, and then roared right alongside the slower boat, rocking its striped awnings and shaking its passengers.

'Cor!' said the small boy in the bows. 'I wish we was on a boat as fast as that one.'

Juan's comment was less repeatable. He turned to shake his fist at the power-boat. There was just one man at the wheel, but the boat had moved away too rapidly for Juan's shout to reach him.

The tourists were shifting uncomfortably on their wooden benches. Lucy tried to think of a joke to cheer them up. But she had hardly started to apologise again when the power-boat rounded them once more, cutting just as close in front of the *San Felipe*, and thudding down its side.

'This is outrageous!' roared a fat middle-aged Englishman, jumping to his feet.

'Please sit down, ladies and gentlemen,' Lucy said desperately. 'I think it must just be a rival tour-boat operator, playing a joke on us.'

'You must do something!' shouted the Englishman.

But what could they do? Lucy asked herself. Aggressive power-boat captains were even less amenable to reason than sports-car drivers. There were no harbour police within sight, and, though the power-boat was upsetting, it was not really being driven dangerously enough to merit a police warning.

The boat rounded on them again, and Juan, wrenching the wheel, pulled the *San Felipe* a little further from the shore.

The power-boat missed them by a wider margin this time, and Juan kept steering diagonally across the empty channel. The boat roared round once more, like a sheepdog herding its flock, and then it arced away, and appeared to cut back to its original mooring.

Lucy heaved a sigh of relief. But there was a great deal of work ahead of her, she could see: all the passengers were upset, and some of them looked decidedly green.

'You'll go to Cala Pedrera?' she asked Juan in Spanish, in an undertone.

Juan nodded. 'We'll settle them there, and then see how it goes.'

'Well, ladies and gentlemen,' Lucy started again, brightly, 'after the excitement I think you might appreciate a quiet bay. We're going to a beautiful inlet called the Cala Pedrera. Maybe some of you know it already: it's within walking distance from the centre of Villa Carlos. The bay's not suitable for children to swim, but adults who are good swimmers can dive from the rocks, and there are some good spots for fishing there. There's a café at the end of the bay, too, so you can cool down with a drink after walking from the town. And talking of drinks....'

She reached for the bottles. A little depressing, she had always thought, that this should be the highlight of the boat trip: but all the passengers welcomed it, and it cost Juan nothing.

'You remember I pointed out to you the gin distillery by Mahon harbourfront? The distillery is open for you to visit, and you're welcome to sample its produce when you call there. But we thought you might just enjoy a little taster now of some of the liqueurs they produce on the island. In this flask I'm passing round a gin cocktail, and this green bottle has an interesting herbal liqueur made with camomile. Do help yourselves, ladies and gentlemen. *Et pour vous, mesdames, un soupçon de cette liqueur de banane ...*'

She offered a bottle of revoltingly sweet banana liqueur to the elderly Frenchwomen, with her most winning smile.

'Hey, Mum, can I ...?'

Lucy swung round rapidly. 'And for the younger passengers, I've some rather nice lemonade,' she added in a loud voice. 'We'll plan to stay here for ten minutes or so, ladies and gentlemen, and then we'll take you round the Lazareto, the big island at the harbour mouth, and back towards Cala Corb, the bay where we embarked. Do keep passing those bottles round, ladies and gentlemen. Let me pass this one up to the far end; this is a very pleasant peppermint liqueur, and the one I'll give to this gentleman in the stern is coffee-flavoured. You can buy all of these, of course, at the distillery, and at many of the super-markets on the island ...'

Two minutes later, all the passengers on the *San Felipe* were talking animatedly over their little plastic glasses of the sticky liqueurs. Lucy grabbed a mo-ment's break, collapsing next to Juan, and gulping down a glassful of the lemonade she had offered to the children.

Usually Juan steered right down the north-eastern shore, through the very narrow channel that separ-ated the Lazareto from the mainland, then out very briefly into the open sea and to the next bay to the west, the Cala St Esteban, where Lucy served the drinks. They had never been forced to change their plans at short notice before. Lucy thought to herself that she would have to watch that nobody drank too much, or some passengers might be sick on the rougher part of the journey; and that they would need to cut short the trip to the other bay, if they were to return at the usual time.

Strange, the incident with the power-boat. It hadn't just been driven carelessly, it had seemed as if the driver was coming deliberately for them. Harassing them; warning them; driving them away from the shoreline.

Why? Lucy couldn't understand it. Juan who everyone's friend, and neither of the boatmen who ran similar trips from Villa Carlos's other bay, Cales Fons, would resort to that type of trick to discourage his customers.

She wondered if Juan had recognised the man at the wheel of the other boat. She knew it wouldn't do to ask him in front of the passengers, though, so instead she picked up her microphone again, and started to hand round bags into which the passengers could put their sticky empty cups, and to tell them the history of the Lazareto, in English and then in French.

The trip seemed almost normal by the time Juan brought the *San Felipe* back into Cala Corb. The little bay was peaceful. The first of the two bars was just beginning to open up for its evening session; a couple of fishermen were looking over their nets at the bayhead; a group of English tourists were clambering over the rocks by the steps that led up to the big hotel, the Don Carlos.

'I do hope you've enjoyed the trip, ladies and gentlemen,' Lucy said into her microphone. 'And if you have, may I recommend to you our other regular trip, on Thursday afternoons and Sunday mornings? We call it a mystery tour, but that's really because the wind and the weather decide for us where we're going to go. We visit a different bay each time, usually one that isn't accessible by land, and give you time to swim and sun yourselves before we journey back again. Did you know, there are over a hundred and twenty different beaches on Minorca? So however long your holiday is, you'll be able to try a new one every day!'

Lucy pushed gently through the passengers to the stern, and jumped on to the harbourside. Juan threw her the mooring rope, and she pulled it in as he edged the boat closer to the water's edge. She propped up the little gangway, hardly more than a plank, that led from the boat to the sloping concrete. Then she stationed herself to help the passengers off, and to make sure they all noticed the shallow dish labelled 'for the captain and the guide'.

When the last of the passengers had disembarked Juan vaulted from the end of the boat, the bags of sticky cups in one hand, and nodded to her, telling her it was time to be getting back to the villa.

Juan was Lucy's uncle by marriage, the husband of her mother's sister Sophie. When Lucy had been looking for a vacation job to fill in the summer before starting her last year at university, Sophie had written to suggest that she come out to Minorca and help them with the boat that they ran each summer season.

She had arrived two months before—and a wonderful two months they had been, full of sun and laughter. She really enjoyed the work. She loved the boat, loved researching the details of Minorca's history for her commentaries, loved practising her languages on the passengers.

Not a cloud in the sky, she thought, until the silly incident that afternoon. But that was what it was, surely, an isolated silly incident. She pushed it firmly from her mind.

Juan and Sophie's house was a modern villa on the outskirts of Villa Carlos, white-walled and red-roofed, with a stunning view down across the main harbour. It was just on seven o'clock by the time Lucy and Juan reached it, and though the sun was still quite high there was a touch of evening cool in the air.

The villa was chaotic, as usual. The kitchen looked like a bomb-site, baby Cara was tired and teary, and six-year-old Manuel and three-year-old Maria seemed somehow to have found another pile of toys to add to the permanent collection scattered around the front room.

Juan cheerfully ignored all the mess, and so did Lucy. She sometimes doubted if Sophie even noticed it. Sophie was always happy, always contented whatever the chaos surrounding her. And, in spite of the apparent havoc in the kitchen, the food—eels in a thick tomato sauce—was glorious.

'You're in tonight, Lucy?' Sophie asked over supper.

Lucy shook her head. 'I'm meeting Vanessa at nine.'

'You'll be back late, then?'

'Not too late.' Late, in Villa Carlos, meant two o'clock or even later. Nobody went to bed early; they all took an afternoon siesta, and revived when the sun went down.

Sophie gave just a hint of a frown. 'I'm sure Liz thinks you're doing more work than you really are, Lucy,' she said.

Liz was Lucy's mother: a headmistress, ten years older than Sophie, and infinitely more disciplined.

Another little cloud drifted across Lucy's blue sky. Her mother certainly imagined that she was knuckling down to her books for several hours a day. But Liz didn't understand what life was like on Minorca, how ill-suited the whole island was to work of that kind. Lucy didn't want to behave like a tourist all summer, and drink and dance every night away, but she did want to see people, and most people were only there to see and be seen after eleven at night. She would have to try and do some more work, she thought, but not that night.

'I'm doing enough,' she said shortly. She got up from the table, feeling slightly annoyed at Sophie for making her feel guilty. 'I've time to bath Cara for you before I go.'

Sophie shook her head. 'She's had a bath and a dip already today. I'll let you off the washing up if you want to work for an hour...'

Lucy gave a wry grin. 'OK. I'll read the next chapter of my economics book, and get ready to go out in double-quick time.'

Vanessa was a tour company representative, based at the Don Carlos, one of the biggest hotels in Villa Carlos. She sold tickets for the *San Felipe* trips at all the hotels on the north-eastern side of the little town; and she joked and gossiped and drank with everybody who passed through the town.

By the time Lucy reached the Don Carlos Vanessa had dried her red hair after her early evening swim, curled it, made up her face, and put on a pretty white sundress with a full skirt and low-cut bodice.

'Very smart,' Lucy said. 'Any special reason? Like a dishy client, say?'

'Lucy, Lucy!' Vanessa scolded. 'You know the rules!'

Lucy grinned. It was one of the things that had drawn her to Vanessa, the fact that the other girl wasn't an inveterate man-chaser like so many of the English girls on Minorca. Vanessa had her rules, and kept to them. Number one: no dating tourists. Instead of haunting the discos looking for a succession of holiday romances she had built up a pleasant circle of friends, some English, some Spanish, among the semi-permanent residents of the island. Lucy was glad to have become one of them.

'I do,' she agreed. 'But every rule gets broken sometimes.'

'Not this time,' Vanessa said firmly. 'Anyway, there was nobody I'd look twice at on the Manchester flight that came in this afternoon. No, actually it was more that I was feeling a bit low, and thought I'd do myself up to compensate. It's been one of those days, lots of niggling complaints about the plumbing and the price of hire cars, and one stupid question after another.'

'I've had one of those too,' Lucy agreed. She glanced past Vanessa into the mirror on the door of her wardrobe. Perhaps she should have made more effort herself, she thought belatedly. The economics textbook hadn't been enthralling, but to still her guilty conscience she had worked hard at it for an hour, and only given herself ten minutes to get ready.

Her hair was all right, she thought critically. She hadn't had the time to put it up, but she had washed it that morning, and it looked pretty good falling loose over her shoulders. It had been bleached even fairer than its usual mid-blonde by the sun, and her tan had deepened to a deep golden brown. Her features were neat, though the contrast with Vanessa didn't flatter her: the other girl had a sharp, gamine face enlivened by blue saucer-eyes and a permanent grin, and in contrast Lucy, with a minimum of make-up, thought she herself looked a little insipid. Her figure was all right, not that you could see much of it under the sage-green boiler-suit she had slipped on. She should have worn something more feminine. Oh, why should she? she thought, exasperated with herself; she wasn't looking for a man, any more than Vanessa was.

'Mal's bar?' Vanessa asked, picking up her bag and slipping on her white sandals.

'Why not? That is, unless the Mancunians have beaten us to it.'

'No chance,' Vanessa said cheerfully. 'I told them all to go to the disco up at the Lady Hamilton.'

They wandered together out through the gardens of the Don Carlos, and down the uneven steps that led from the edge of the hotel grounds to the bay below. It was only nine-fifteen. Early, by Minorcan standards. Mal's bar would be empty, Lucy thought. Still, Mal himself would be there. He would cheer them both up.

Mal ran a typical Minorcan cave bar, one of two in Cala Corb. The tables outside were still empty when Lucy and Vanessa reached it. 'Guitar music and songs from ten-thirty,' announced a placard which sported a photo of Mal looking much, much younger than his real age, and another, more convincing, of Pedro, the boy from Villa Carlos who played guitar in the bar.

They went on inside. The cave was narrow and deep, with a faint smell of wine and cooked sardines. It had a long wooden bar down one side, and tables and benches covered in red vinyl along the other side. Spotlights, their wires trailing across the bare rock of the roof, illuminated niches in the uneven walls which held some of the flotsam that Mal had picked up—mainly, he cheerfully admitted, in the junk shops of Ciudadela rather than from harbour wrecks. Lucy had seen the bar in daytime, and been surprised to discover how scruffy it really was. But by night, with just the spotlights to light it, and Mal's conversation to fill it, it had the relaxed, low-key charm of all the best Minorcan bars.

Mal's conversation was needed to fill the bar just then, for Lucy had guessed right: there was only one other customer. Mal was propping up the bar from the business side, and the customer was sitting on a stool facing him. A dark-haired man, in his early thirties perhaps, wearing jeans and a blindingly white shirt, its sleeves turned up to show off tanned forearms.

Both men turned as the girls entered. A pair of deep brown eyes connected with Lucy's green ones. They held her gaze for a moment, then she looked away, disconcerted by her response to the man's look, and towards Mal.

'Vanessa, my darling!' squealed Mal, coming out from behind the bar in their honour, and giving Vanessa a generous bear-hug. 'Looking absolutely ravishing tonight, I may say. And the lovely Lucy, too.' He bestowed a deep bow on her. 'My dears, you haven't been in for days!'

'Mal, darling, we're in the bay every day.' Vanessa grinned. 'But hardly ever at the same time as you are.'

'My loss, my dears, my loss entirely. Now, what can I do for you?'

Lucy slipped on to a stool, three away from the dark-haired man. She cast him a sideways glance, then hurriedly turned away again. It might look as if she was inviting him to buy her a drink, she thought, and she certainly wasn't intending to do that. She wasn't interested in picking up men in bars.

'Two soda waters, please, Mal,' she said.

'One soda water,' Vanessa corrected. 'And a glass of white wine. Or shall we make it two of those, Lucy? You said you'd had a rough day too, I reckon you could do with it.'

'I guess I could. OK, Mal, two glasses of wine.'

'My pleasure, dears.' Mal busied himself pouring the wine, and Vanessa turned to the other man.

'Now you,' she said brightly, 'are definitely not one of mine.'

'One of yours?'

Lucy felt herself going scarlet—on Vanessa's account. Did Vanessa always have to talk to every stranger she met? she thought, irritated, forgetting momentarily that she had always admired Vanessa's outgoing nature. Did Vanessa have to use such an awful phrase? Lucy knew it wasn't intended as a blatant come-on, but what on earth must the man think?

Whatever he thought, he didn't make it apparent, and Vanessa went on, 'My clients, I mean. Gosh, that did sound a bit odd, didn't it? But you see, I always remember their faces. And you didn't come in on the Manchester flight or the Luton flight, did you?'

'No. No, I didn't.'

'There, I knew it!' Vanessa responded triumphantly. She held out a hand. 'Vanessa Jenkins. I mother all the Worldair clients at the Don Carlos hotel. Anything you need to know about Villa Carlos, just ask me.'

'Now, now, Vanessa,' Mal scolded. 'I just told my friend here to ask *me* to tell him anything he needs to know.'

'Then I shall ask you both,' the man responded politely. 'Not that there is anything I wish to know right now.'

Mal raised an eyebrow at this, Lucy noticed. She glanced at the bartop, and saw that there were two half-empty glasses on it, besides their own full glasses of wine. So the stranger had bought Mal a drink. And he had been asking Mal questions before they arrived, she was sure; but now he evidently did not plan to ask any more.

'Or you could ask Lucy, come to that,' Vanessa continued cheerily. 'Her special subject's the harbour history, but she's not bad on the shops and bars either. And she's great on bus timetables.'

Lucy flushed again. What an introduction!

The stranger had dropped Vanessa's hand, and was holding his out to her. She took it. He had a cool, firm grip, she noticed, and long fingers. She kept looking at his fingers, suddenly reluctant to meet those brown eyes again.

'Laurent,' he said in a low voice.

Laurent. A French name. But no French accent that she had noticed. Lucy raised her eyes a little, and looked him over.

The jeans were an expensive make, well-cut, tight-fitting. The shirt was new, surely, and also fitted well. The body under them was long; he must be very tall, standing up. He was on the slender side. It was a conservative outfit, conservatively worn: no playboy expanses of hairy chest, no medallions, no flashy rings. No clues to his nationality. Except that she had assumed he was English, and she so rarely made that mistake.

Her eyes came last to his face. It was a slim face too, with finely cut features. Patrician, distinguished. A firm chin, a straight nose, a widish straight mouth. His hair was short, well cut. And those eyes—she met their gaze again, and felt a little shock pass through her.

There was no denying it. He was devastatingly attractive.

'Lucy's the guide on the *San Felipe*,' Mal said. 'Her harbour tours are not to be missed. Daily, at ... two-thirty, is it, Lucy?'

Lucy came to her senses. She'd been staring at him. And she'd been so absorbed in what she saw that she hadn't even introduced herself properly, so that Mal had had to do it for her.

'Three-thirty.' She dutifully corrected what was surely Mal's deliberate mistake. 'Not an hour at which Mal is ever awake.'

'But then you, my dear, are rarely awake at three-thirty in the morning.'

'How true. God, I'll be dead by eleven tonight!' Vanessa groaned loudly, claimed one of the stools between Lucy and Laurent, and set her head down on the bartop.

'Rough day, you said?' Mal prompted.

'Rough? Coarse sandpaper all the way!' Vanessa lifted her head, took a hefty gulp of the wine, and launched into a hilarious account of the customers who had dragged her into their bathroom and urged her to sample the temperature of the bathwater for herself.

By the time she reached the end of the tale, Lucy had relaxed enough to laugh with Mal and Laurent. So what, she told herself, if he *was* the most gorgeous man she'd met all summer? Why did that have to upset her? She ought to be enjoying a flirtation with him, not trembling at every glance.

Lucy had her rules, just as Vanessa did: lots of fun, but no love-them-and-leave-them holiday romances. But she didn't have to break the rules for Laurent, she reminded herself. Things need go no further than she chose. She would probably never see him again anyway. There was no harm in spending an evening looking and admiring. No harm in meeting those brown eyes, no harm in enjoying that prickle of awareness that ran down her spine.

'So what was your disaster, Lucy?' Vanessa asked.

Disaster? No, meeting this man wasn't a disaster. Just a pleasant diversion. She frowned.

'You'd had a tough day too, you said?'

Of course—it was her turn to amuse them with tales of her ghastly clients. For the first time in hours, Lucy remembered the power-boat.

'A bit up and down,' she said, temporising. Meanwhile, she was thinking fast. Should she tell them the story? It wasn't the kind of anecdote they expected, and, though it had been quite a trivial incident, it could have genuinely unpleasant repercussions. She didn't want to spread any tales that might affect the *San Felipe*'s bookings.

'Up and down?' Mal echoed. 'The water's been as smooth as a millpond today.'

'It should have been,' Lucy agreed. 'But actually we had a bit of trouble with a power-boat....'

She suppressed her lingering doubts and went on with the tale, trying to keep it light and bantering. She didn't want Laurent to think her boring in comparison with Vanessa, she told herself. Actually he didn't. He wasn't interested in Vanessa, she could tell. His eyes had been on her all the time.

She could sense him concentrating as she spoke. It interested him, her tale about the odd goings-on in the harbour. No, she told herself, that wasn't it at all. Of course he wasn't particularly interested in the stupid story; it was rather that he was so evidently attracted to the girl who was telling it.

'Weird,' Vanessa said as she finished.

Lucy gave a light shrug. 'I thought it was odd at the time, but now I can see that there couldn't really have been anything behind it. It was just a joke, I expect. All the same, though, it did seem like an odd kind of joke to play.'

'You ought to check with Anna,' Mal said. 'She'd be able to tell you if the *Blue Boat* or any of the others have had the same sort of thing happen to them.'

'I'm sure there's no need to do that,' Laurent said. 'It sounds like an isolated incident to me. A drunken tourist, perhaps. I think you would do better to forget it.'

It was the first time he had spoken for several minutes. Lucy glanced at him. He sounded very certain, very reassuring. He was right. She ought to forget it. She *had* forgotten it. Heavens, she wouldn't even have mentioned it if Vanessa hadn't reminded her.

'I shall,' she agreed. 'It's forgotten already. Now it's your turn, Laurent. Did anything strange happen to you today?'

Laurent smiled and shrugged his shoulders. It was a nice smile, but it didn't seem to reach his eyes. Lucy thought, momentarily, that he was annoyed by her question. But it was quite reasonable of her, surely; she and Vanessa had entertained him, why shouldn't he entertain them in turn?

'To be honest,' he said, 'I hadn't left my villa all day until I came here this evening. So I'm afraid I have no funny stories to relate.'

'Spoilsport,' Vanessa said, but in a friendly voice. 'Where's your villa, Laurent?'

'Just outside Mahon.'

That was vague, very vague. Vanessa obviously thought so too. 'This side of the harbour?' she pursued.

'No, the other side.'

'On the waterfront?'

'Actually it is, yes.'

'You can't have been far from where the power-boat drove at the *San Felipe*, then. See anything?'

Vanessa's questioning was still friendly, but it was obvious to Lucy by now that Laurent was annoyed. His answers were as short as he could politely make them. 'No,' he said.

'Pity. You might have solved the mystery for us.'

'I only wish I could help,' Laurent said. 'But I am afraid I know nothing about it.' He reached for his glass, and emptied it. 'So nice to have met you, ladies.'

'Drop in again some time,' Mal called after him as he left.

There was a silence. The bar seemed very quiet. There were still no other customers, though that was nothing unusual: things would liven up considerably after ten.

'You annoyed him, Vanessa,' Mal said thoughtfully.

'Can't see why,' Vanessa replied. 'Sorry if I drove him away, though, Lucy.'

'Sorry?'

'Well, I thought maybe you . . .'

'Oh, no!' Lucy hastily responded. 'Shall we have another drink?'

Vanessa fumbled for her purse. And Lucy thought, suddenly, it couldn't have been Laurent, could it, who was steering the power-boat? No. Of course it couldn't have been.

CHAPTER TWO

AT A QUARTER past eleven in the morning, Lucy dashed down the steps from the Don Carlos hotel to Cala Corb, with a T-shirt pulled on over her damp bikini. She had been up to the hotel to retrieve Vanessa's takings and unsold tickets for the afternoon trip, and had lingered to swim in the pool. The staff all knew her, and were happy to let her use it.

The bay was almost deserted: there were only a couple of tourists in sight, and half a dozen fishermen—including Juan. Lucy could see from the steps that Juan had finished mending his fishing-nets. When she reached him she panted an apology for getting back late. He wasn't annoyed with her, but he stayed only to check on the ticket situation before disappearing with a couple of the other fishermen.

Lucy went to fill a bucket with water from a tap on the quay, and started on the first of her daily jobs—cleaning out the drinks locker on the *San Felipe*.

A couple of tourists drifted down to the bay and bought tickets as she was finishing her work. Then she went to sit in the sun by the notice advertising that day's mystery tour. She pulled the T-shirt off over her head again, and settled down on a folding chair with a book, keeping half an eye and ear open for customers.

The bay slowly grew busier. The second of the two cave bars, the Illa Plana, opened for lunch as well as supper, and the barman clattered down to the harbour and set about unlocking and distributing his tables on the quayside. Lucy talked to him for a few minutes, bought a Coke from him, sold three more tickets, and thought wistfully of the pool on the clifftop above her. Some small boys came down the steps with fishing-rods and plastic buckets; a few tourists appeared from round the promontory, hot after the scramble over the rocks, and headed for the bar. A couple of boatmen took their boats out, nodding to Lucy as they set off.

She read a few more pages of her book. It was a course book, heavy-going. Too early for her to eat her sandwiches. The sun made her drowsy. Her eyes half shut.

'Miss!' She was started awake by a deep male voice.

She turned to face its owner. He turned out to be a swarthy man, rather plump, with a heavy trace of beard, wearing the shapeless trousers and brownish shirt that were almost an uniform for the younger fishermen. He didn't strike her as a likely buyer of tickets for the mystery tour.

'Yes?'

'The boat? *San Felipe?* It is yours?'

'My uncle's.' Lucy frowned. The man was speaking Catalan, with a Minorcan accent so thick that she found it hard to follow him. She spoke quite good Castilian, standard Spanish, but only a little of the Catalan that had, since the end of General Franco's era, become the main language on the island.

'Tell your uncle to keep away from the villas,' the man said. 'You tell him, it is not good to sail your boat so close to the shore. The owners of the villas over there, they don't like it.' He gestured across the harbour. 'You tell him, he is to keep away.'

Lucy's frown deepened. 'I don't understand,' she said slowly. 'Who are you? Who sent you here?'

'You tell him,' repeated the man. 'The boats, they must keep to this side of the harbour. It is not good to sail close to the villas. You tell him.'

Lucy stared at him. What a strange thing to say. What was he saying this for, what was he doing in Cala Corb? She suddenly felt apprehensive. She was at a disadvantage, sitting in the low folding chair while he loomed over her. She pushed herself out of it, and moved a pace away from him. 'You do this thing, you have no trouble,' the man said.

And if they didn't do as he suggested? Heavens, this was a threat! Lucy glanced sideways. The fishermen had all disappeared for their lunch and siesta. There were a few tourists eating outside the bar, but there was nobody she knew in sight, nobody she could call on to come to her rescue.

'I think you ought to come back when my uncle is here,' she said, rather lamely.

The man did not react. 'You tell him,' he repeated. He stood there for a moment, glaring at her, then turned away and strode off down the side of the bay.

Lucy watched him, mesmerised. He passed along the row of moored boats. Then he stopped near the end of the row, jumped into one of the boats, and started to cast off.

It was a white power-boat. Good heavens, Lucy thought, it must be the one that had harried the *San Felipe* the day before!

The man started the engine, and roared out of the bay, and away across the harbour.

Lucy stared blindly at the wake that spread across the bay. Keep away from the villas. It began to make sense. This man had surely been driving the power-boat the day before, and it was obvious to her now that that was what he had been doing: trying to keep the *San Felipe* well clear of the villas on the harbourfront. And now he had come in person to reinforce his message.

He couldn't own one of the villas, surely? He didn't look remotely like one of the rich international set who lived along the waterfront. She thought he must work for one of the owners—so it would be his master, surely, who had given him instructions to keep the pleasure-boats away from his villa and grounds?

Lucy was not frightened, not now the man had gone. But, now he *had* gone, she discovered she was thoroughly angry. What a cheek! A harbour was like a road: you couldn't stop people using it, even if they did come too close for convenience. Juan and the other pleasure-boat owners had been doing the harbour tour for years. They would hardly change course just because some rich resident found them a nuisance.

It struck her, rather too late, that she should have said this to him. Well, maybe not; he had looked awfully strong and aggressive, and she wouldn't have liked to risk antagonising him too much. Juan should have been there, and said it to him. Juan would say it to him, if he persisted in this strange campaign. Because, Lucy told herself, she and Juan wouldn't dream of giving in to his threats; they wouldn't change the San Felipe's course one inch.

'Do?' asked Juan. 'Why, we do nothing. We wait to see what happens.'

Sophie added, 'Anyway, there's nothing we can do. A plumpish, ill-shaven, dark man in working clothes. How on earth could we ever find out who he was? There must be thousands of men like that around here.'

They were sitting over supper, that evening. There had been no new trouble on the afternoon's boat trip: not surprisingly, because for the mystery tour the *San Felipe* had not passed anywhere near the villas on the north-east side of the harbour. But Lucy had convinced herself, thinking it over that afternoon, that Juan ought to do something about the veiled threat she had received.

'I know it would be hard to trace him,' she agreed. 'I know there are dozens of white-painted power-boats just like the one I saw. I wish I'd noticed the name on the boat yesterday. I couldn't read it today, it was too far off, but it was the same boat, I'm certain of it.'

Juan said, 'I should have read the name, but I didn't.'

'So?'

'You really want to do something? Well, if you are determined, maybe you could ask Anna and Jaime. Perhaps he has rocked the *Blue Boat* too. Anna could tell you, and if so, there's a good chance that she would have noticed the boat's name.'

That was the advice Mal had given her, to ask Anna. It made sense to Lucy. If the Minorcan was serious about keeping the pleasure-boats away from the shore, she thought, then he would surely have tackled the other boat owners, too. 'I'll do that in the morning,' she said.

The *Blue Boat* was based in Cales Fons, the larger of the two bays around which Villa Carlos was built. Lucy made her way there the next morning, to the bar where the tickets for the boat were sold.

Anna was a lively woman from Barcelona. She was sitting at one of the tables outside the bar, painting her fingernails scarlet.

'Hello, Anna,' said Lucy, sitting down opposite her. 'Juan suggested I talk to you. Have you and Jaime had any trouble recently with a power-boat in the harbour?'

Anna's eyes narrowed. She reached out with a red-taloned hand and carefully picked up the little bottle of varnish. 'Come inside,' she said.

Lucy followed her to the depths of the bar. Anna sat down in a low wicker chair, and deposited the varnish on a glass-topped table.

'So Juan had trouble, too,' she said.

'On Wednesday. We didn't do the harbour trip yesterday, so I don't know if the power-boat was back then.'

'It wasn't, no, but we were harassed by it on Wednesday, just as you were. It's the *Santa Caterina*. Jaime knows the man who used to own it, but he sold it a couple of months ago to a boatyard in Mahon.'

'Could you tell which villa he came from?'

Anna shook her head. 'He took off from a long wooden quay that's shared by four villas.'

'Four!'

'That's right. The end one is owned by a singer from Barcelona, but she's been coming to the island for years, and she's not the kind to make trouble.' Anna named her: a singer of popular ballads, well known for her relaxed style. 'Then there's a bigger villa that changed hands a year or so ago. Easy to spot, it's on three levels, set right into the hillside. It belongs to a French banker now, I'd heard. Nobody famous. Then there's a green-painted villa that belongs to the owner of a nightclub in Mahon, and the last one with access to the quay is owned by a retired English couple.'

'A nightclub owner,' Lucy said.

'That's right. He's had dealings with the island police once or twice. And there was a rumour last summer that the Madrid drug squad had sent a man to the island to investigate him.'

Drug squad! Lucy shivered. But perhaps it wasn't the nightclub owner, she told herself.

'And the English couple?' she asked. 'Perhaps we could ask them about their neighbours, see if anyone has mentioned a crackdown on the pleasure-boats to them.'

Anna spread her red fingers. 'You know the English,' she said. 'They stay on the island all winter, when sensible people leave it to the gales, then come summer they rent out their villas and go home to rainy England.'

Lucy laughed. She didn't think it all that silly of the English, but it was true, she had to admit: they did seem to be the only nationality that behaved in that way.

'So Jaime plans to check up on the power-boat first?' she asked.

Anna hesitated. 'He could ask at the boatyard, I suppose—but I do not think he will bother. Why look for work? We can move a little further out towards midstream when we come up to the quay. It will all be forgotten in a week or so. By next season we shall have drifted back to our old course.'

'But the man had no right to threaten us like that!' Lucy protested.

'It is not nice, but what else is there to do?'

There had to be something they could do. They could talk to the police; they could make enquiries themselves. But Jaime was just like Juan, Lucy thought to herself. Lazy, gentle, not one to go looking for trouble, or to exert himself unnecessarily.

All the same, though Juan and Jaime seemed to think it wasn't necessary to do anything, Lucy still wasn't sure that she agreed.

She said, 'If one villa owner persuades us to change course, others might do the same.'

Anna shrugged. 'If they do, we will think again.' She glanced across the table, and saw Lucy's expression. 'Ah, the English sense of fair play! You want the man to be punished.'

'Not punished, exactly,' Lucy said. 'Well—yes, I suppose I would like that. I just don't think we should let him get away with it.'

'Lucy, my dear, many people get away with much worse deeds than that one!'

Lucy laughed with Anna. But at the same time she was annoyed—and curious. Who was it, she wondered, who was so anxious to keep the pleasure-boats further away? And why? Was it no more than an obsessive sense of privacy? But the villa owners all knew, surely, that it was a hazard of waterfront life that a continual stream of strangers would sail past the foot of their garden. There was a mystery here, and she wanted to get to the bottom of it.

She said goodbye to Anna and drifted across to Cala Corb, working out a plan as she went.

Juan was working on the *San Felipe*'s engine.

'I'll be here all morning,' he said. 'You go off, if you want, until two-thirty.'

'You don't need help, Juan?'

He grinned. 'You'd be in my way, lass.'

'May I take the *Sophie*?' That was a little dinghy with an outboard motor, that Juan used for fishing.

'Fill up the tank first. There's some bait in the hut if you want to fish.'

'Thanks, Juan.' Lucy went to the little hut where Juan kept his nets and supplies. She located a petrol can, the light fishing-rod she generally used herself, a tobacco tin with spare hooks and floats, a plastic bag, and a plastic jar half-full of snail bait. She put these in the *Sophie*, added her sandwiches and a can of fizzy orange, checked the motor, peeled off her shorts—though she left her floppy white T-shirt on over her bikini—and with a wave to Juan set off down the bay.

She hadn't told Juan where she was planning to go. Or even that she was going to fish, though he obviously imagined that she was. She might as well, she

thought: it would be good camouflage. The fishing
would probably be as good just off the long wooden
quay at the far side of the harbour as in any of the
small bays she usually frequented.

She veered up the main harbour, to take the dinghy
out of Juan's line of sight—not that she expected him
to look where she was going—and then cut across the
main ship channel as soon as it was clear. Her course
brought her about half a mile south-east of the row
of villas she was aiming for. She worked slowly up
towards them, keeping in the lee of the moored yachts,
until she caught sight of the green-painted villa Anna
had mentioned.

There were three boats tied up by the long wooden
quay. That didn't surprise her. Every villa household
owned at least one boat, and in midsummer they rarely
bothered to return them to the boathouses. She
chugged past, looking carefully at them. There were
a couple of dinghies much like the *Sophie*, and a small
yacht, chrome-railed and gleaming. There was no sign
of the white power-boat.

No yachts were anchored in the stretch of water just
beyond the quay. Presumably the scruffy Minorcan
had shooed them all out of range. Lucy thought,
uneasily, that she would look more conspicuous than
she had bargained. But it was not so strange for
somebody to stop in a quiet stretch of water like that
one; and her fishing-rod would provide a convincing
excuse.

She cut the outboard motor a few yards upstream,
and the *Sophie* drifted to a halt. There was hardly any
current in the harbour; even without an anchor the
dinghy would not move far. She reached for the tackle

tin and the snails, cracked open a snailshell on the side of the boat, and began to thread its contents on to a hook.

She was more nervous than she had admitted to herself; it took three casts before she had the line set decently. Then she settled down comfortably on the bench of the dinghy and waited.

Anna knew the harbour so well, she thought to herself. The row of villas was exactly as she had described it. The high-sided, white-painted villa, with a veranda facing away from the harbour, surely belonged to the singer. It was completely shuttered: she must be back on the mainland. Then there was the low, three-level villa. That was occupied: the awnings were set at the windows, washing flapped on a line, but nobody was in sight. Then the smart green villa, the railings down its steps newly painted white, its name-sign surrounded with coloured lights. And up from the last set of steps that led to the wooden quay, the rather plain villa belonging to the retired English couple. A family must have rented it; Lucy could hear children shouting from the terrace and pool.

Absorbed in checking over the coastline, she missed the first tug on her line. By the time she had reeled it in, the fish had escaped. Sighing, she set another snail on the hook and casted again.

It was hypnotic, watching the little red and white float bob up and down on the wavelets. The Palma ferry steamed past, and the dinghy and the float rocked in its wake. The wake was still dying away when the float disappeared under the waves, and Lucy— alert this time—hauled hard on her rod.

Not very elegantly, she succeeded in landing a
rainbow fish in the dinghy. Maybe half a pound—
hardly a record breaker, but a good start to the
morning. She had just stowed it in the plastic bag when
a slight movement caught her eye on the hillside, and
she turned abruptly towards the villas.

A man was standing in the garden of the low white
villa, the one Anna had said belonged to a French
banker. He was on a small terrace, perhaps midway
between the villa itself and the quay, that was obviously reached from the steps that led down to the
quay.

He hadn't been there when she had looked half an
hour earlier. No, on second thoughts, he probably
had. Sitting down, he would have been just out of
her line of sight. She must have exclaimed when the
fish bit, or simply made enough commotion with the
rod and line to have caught his attention, and he had
stood up to see what was going on out in the harbour.

He was too far away from her to see him well, but
she was sure he wasn't the scruffy Minorcan who had
threatened her in Cala Corb. This man was taller and
slighter, though he too was dark-haired and very
tanned. He was wearing only a pair of white shorts.

Since he was obviously watching her—and she had
just as obviously noticed him—she smiled and waved
in his direction; and then, for good measure, picked
up the plastic bag and held it at arm's length, showing
off its not very impressive contents.

The man did not react. Lucy dropped the bag back
into the bottom of the dinghy, and reached for the
bait jar. Out of the corner of her eye, she could see
that the man on the hillside had moved now; he

seemed to be making for the steps. She thought then that he might well be the Minorcan's employer. If so, perhaps he was coming down to the quay to talk to her, to ask her to move further away.

That was what she wanted, wasn't it? To find out who was behind the threats, to have a chance to reason with whoever it was? Her stomach seemed to be leaping inside her. She didn't actually want a confrontation, she thought nervously, just to know a little more.

She turned sideways on to the quay, her back to the foot of the steps, as she fumbled for the hook. Perhaps that would discourage him from calling out to her. She tried to watch the quay from the corner of her eye as she threaded some new bait on to her hook.

She stood up in the dinghy, feet splayed, and prepared to cast the line. Her shoulders and arms had just come back for the cast when the white powerboat roared across her bows.

The *Sophie* tipped violently, as the other boat's wake slammed into her. Lucy, off balance because of the rod, tipped even more violently. The fishing-rod shot out of her hands. Instinctively she reached out to grab it, and as the dinghy rocked back again she found herself heading inevitably for the water.

She met it head-first. Her belly hit a moment later, and her feet tumbled in last of all. It wasn't a bad dive, in the circumstances—a bit uncontrolled; she went a long way down before she managed to pull herself together. There was an unearthly moment when she was drifting through the cold green depths, disorientated; then she gave a little kick, and took a stroke back towards the surface.

Only one, because then strong hands grabbed her by the shoulders. She lashed out instinctively. Her assailant's grip tightened into a classic lifesaving hold, and her arm flailed past him.

Lifesaving. He had dived in to help her. Damn him, whoever he was; she felt enough of a fool falling in, without having somebody there to make a real drama out of it. She was a strong swimmer, and felt she had been in no real danger, but there was no arguing with that strong, professional grip, so she went limp and let him haul her to the surface.

Once she got there she spluttered, and spat out a mouthful of seawater. She couldn't see; her hair hung in a wet curtain across her face, and neither arm was free to move it. The man holding her dragged her for a few short strokes, and then came to an abrupt stop. He reached for her arm, and guided her hand to something solid.

At the same time he loosed her other arm, and she was able to move her hair out of her eyes and see where she was. She was holding one of the struts of the wooden quay. They must have surfaced in the narrow expanse of water between it and the *Sophie*.

'There are steps,' said the man. 'Can you get to them?'

'Of course I can,' snapped Lucy, without looking at him. Fortunately the steps were on the other side of her to her rescuer. She let go of the strut, and swam the short distance to them.

It was harder work than she had anticipated, swimming those few strokes unaided and hauling herself up the wooden steps and out of the water. She collapsed in an ungainly heap on the quay, and hardly noticed the man following her out of the water.

He stood there for a moment, towering over her, and then reached out to draw her to her feet.

Lucy pulled her arm away from his, angrily, as soon as she was upright. Curse her unsteadiness! It was just the shock of the impact. The water had felt colder than it usually seemed when she went swimming in the harbour. She was shivering. She wrapped her arms around herself, and glared at her rescuer.

Oh, no! Not Laurent.

It was very definitely Laurent. A very wet Laurent, wearing nothing but a pair of sodden white shorts, and looking at her with a mixture of annoyance and concern which made her feel weak and furious, all at the same time.

So much, thought Lucy, for my conviction that I wasn't going to see him again.

She tried to think of something to say. She was damned if she would thank him. She hadn't asked to be rescued, and come to that she hadn't needed to be rescued. Then she thought, so he is the French banker Anna mentioned. Of course. A thousand to one, he's the man behind the threats.

The things she thought of saying then were totally unrepeatable.

In the end she just said, 'The boat...'

'Alonzo has her.'

Laurent turned from Lucy and looked out to the water. Lucy followed his gaze. A plumpish swarthy man who was presumably Alonzo was pulling the *Sophie* by its mooring rope towards the white power-

boat. He was, of course, the man who had accosted
her at Cala Corb.

Laurent went to the edge of the quay. Alonzo
brought the two boats alongside, and Laurent reached
out to catch their ropes and moor them securely.

Lucy found herself ignored. She took the opportunity to wring a stream of water out of her hair.

Still nobody was paying any attention to her, so she
wrung another river from the hem of her T-shirt. At
least the water was fairly clean, she thought: but she
could scarcely have looked more of a wreck than she
did.

She cast a cautious glance at the men. Though the
sight of Alonzo was unnerving enough, her eyes were
drawn, irresistibly, to Laurent. He was sleek as a seal
after his sudden ducking, with his short hair plastered
to his head and droplets of water glistening on his
bare back. The muscles rippled under his skin as he
heaved on the rope. He might be a slender man, but
he was fit and strong, thought Lucy, remembering the
iron-hard grip that had caught her under the water.

Soon both boats were firmly secured to mooring
rings. Lucy had watched all this operation before it
dawned on her that she had absolutely no wish for
the *Sophie* to be moored at Laurent's quay. She
couldn't face confronting him over the *San Felipe* just
then, not when she was soaking wet, and shivering
still. She had an increasingly powerful urge to be back
in the dinghy, and chugging back over the channel as
fast as the little outboard motor would carry her.

She moved a pace or two towards the dinghy. Then
she remembered the fishing-rod. It was Juan's rod that

she had borrowed: not one of his best, but she could hardly go back without it.

It had to be in the water: floating, with luck. She peered at the surface, and thought she saw a longish shape that caught the sun, and might be varnished wood.

She moved a step sideways, to place herself by the free expanse of water between the boats, and prepared to dive in and retrieve it.

Laurent's arm caught her in mid-lunge. It landed across her chest, and hauled her firmly backwards, until she was trapped tight against his hard body.

'What on earth,' he said, in a cold voice, 'do you think you're doing?'

Lucy struggled to free herself, and finally managed to get him to loosen his grip.

'I'm hardly planning to commit suicide,' she said sarcastically. 'I need to get the rod back. It isn't mine, I borrowed it.'

'You cannot possibly dive into that water again. You're still shaken. And you'd be wasting your time, anyway. It's broken.'

'Oh, no!' Lucy exclaimed.

'Oh, yes. Leave it and come up to the house.'

'Oh, no!' Lucy repeated, in a different tone this time.

'Oh, yes,' Laurent said firmly. He took her arm, and led her determinedly towards the steps.

Lucy was beyond argument. Alonzo was not. He followed them all the way up the hillside, with a torrent of Catalan pouring of him at every step. Lucy scarcely listened to it. She knew what he was telling Laurent: that she was the guide from the *San Felipe*, that he had been doing his damnedest to keep her well away from the villa, and that he was not at all amused to see his hard work go rewarded in such a way.

Laurent paid him no attention until they stopped at a courtyard. Then he turned, still holding Lucy's arm in a tight grip, and said, 'I told you before to speak Castilian to me. Go and ask Juana to find towels for the young lady.'

Alonzo went. That was a relief.

Laurent led Lucy across the courtyard and through a pair of glass doors, into a living-room. She scarcely took in its appearance. There was a sofa. As soon as he released her she subsided on to this.

She didn't notice what Laurent was doing until he came to squat in front of her, and closed her fingers around the stem of a glass.

There was the unmistakable smell of brandy.

'Drink this,' he said. 'No arguments.'

Lucy gazed helplessly at him. He was very close to her. His fingers felt warm against hers. She couldn't avoid his eyes.

And here she was, soaking wet, sitting in his villa and about to drink his brandy. Except that he was the French banker, and he was behind the threats to the *San Felipe*.

'No. No, really.' She thought of standing up, but she couldn't do that without touching him. 'There's absolutely no need for this. I swim in the harbour every day.'

'No doubt. But right now you are in shock. Look, your hand is trembling.'

The little amber puddle of brandy in the glass was indeed mirroring the shivering of Lucy's hand, Lucy's arm. Lucy looked at it, and thought that she ought to take off the wet T-shirt. She couldn't imagine doing that, not with Laurent watching her.

His hand guided hers up to her mouth, and she took a sip of the brandy. It slid down her like fire.

'That's better. Now here is Juana with the towels.'

Laurent got to his feet. Lucy watched him cross the room to the doorway where a Minorcan woman, youngish, short and fat, had appeared with a large armful of white towels. He talked to her in Castilian. He clearly spoke it fluently. He was asking her to show Lucy to a bathroom.

Lucy got to her feet. Her legs held her more steadily this time.

'Look,' she said, 'this is awfully kind of you, but there really is no need for it. I'll dry in the sun in no time.'

'Nonsense. It is no trouble. Juana will show you where you can clean up. I'll see you in the courtyard in a few minutes.'

He had such a confident manner, Lucy thought to herself. He must be used to people doing exactly what he told them to do. She couldn't imagine defying him successfully. And the longer she stayed shivering in the room, the more tempting the idea of a warm shower sounded.

She followed Juana. The woman led her to a small white-tiled bathroom. Presumably it was a guest bathroom: it was spotless and anonymous, but equipped with soap, shampoo and even a comb. Lucy locked the door as soon as Juana had gone. She stripped off her sodden T-shirt and bikini, and switched on the shower.

Laurent's villa had unusually efficient plumbing, by Minorcan standards. The water ran hot almost immediately. The shower was so highly pressurised that it prickled on her skin. Lucy lingered under the jet. It was the most delicious shower she could ever remember.

She didn't start to think coherently about the situation until she was rubbing herself dry on part of the vast collection of towels that Juana had deposited. Then her mind suddenly clicked into gear, and began to run faster, and faster.

What had she told Laurent in Mal's bar? It was important that she remember exactly what she had said. She had made a joke of the power-boat incident, admittedly. But he must have realised that it was Alonzo who had harassed the *San Felipe*. He must have given orders to Alonzo to do that. What had *he* said in the bar, when she told the story? Nothing that she could remember, except that she should forget it.

Forget it? Forget the *San Felipe* being rocked by the power-boat, forget Alonzo threatening her on the quay? All right, it was hardly first degree murder, but it wasn't a matter to be forgotten, either.

Juan thought it was, a voice in her head told her. And Sophie, and Anna, and Jamie. No matter. Lucy Sanderson thought it wasn't.

No wonder he had been annoyed, she went on to herself, when Vanessa had asked him where his villa was. I even thought to myself that it might have been him steering the power-boat. Well, it wasn't—I think—but it was close enough. He was behind it, no doubt about that.

And now she was going to have to confront him properly, indebted to him for a glass of brandy and many gallons of hot water, not to mention a pile of clean towels, and wearing nothing but the sodden bikini that was lying on the bathroom floor.

She picked it up. It was a very small yellow bikini. She had been wearing it all summer, and always thought it perfectly respectable—more than respectable, when many of the women around her were going topless. Looking at it now, it seemed awfully insubstantial. Wet, it was almost transparent. She checked her appearance in the mirror after she had fastened the top on, and saw that her nipples were clearly outlined under the damp fabric.

So what? she told herself. Her body was nothing to be ashamed of. On the contrary, she could be proud of it: it was smooth-skinned, supple and fit, its curves gently but unmistakably feminine. If Laurent found her attractive, she ought to be able to use that as a weapon against him.

Except that she hadn't wanted to fight him. That was the horrible thing, that she had thought him so attractive, had thought him likeable, and now she knew that he employed Alonzo and he was responsible for the harassing of the pleasure-boats.

She looked around on the floor for the T-shirt. No, she couldn't put that back until it was dry. Wet, it wouldn't act as much of a cover-up anyway. There was a towelling bathrobe hanging on the door, but she didn't like the thought of putting that on. She would have to take it off again before she left, and she had a vague idea that she might need to make a quick getaway if things became nasty.

Nasty? Well, they could, she thought, remembering Alonzo and his aggressive manner on the quay. No, surely they wouldn't, not here. She combed her hair quickly, conscious that she had taken an appallingly long time over the shower, and went out of the bathroom, and in search of Laurent.

CHAPTER THREE

It was a very big villa, larger than it had looked from the harbour. And it was not just on three levels, as Anna had said, but on half a dozen or more. Lucy wandered through a seemingly endless series of interconnecting rooms, each a few steps up or down from the next. Finally she realised that the corridor she was walking along led right around the outside of the house, and that she needed to cut through one of the rooms off it in order to reach the courtyard.

She opened a door, and went into a bedroom—one not in use, thank goodness, from the look of it. Did Laurent live alone? she couldn't help wondering. The opposite wall was all of glass, with a sliding door set into it, and a view beyond of the courtyard that she was looking for.

The door, when she tried it, was unlocked, and she stepped cautiously out. The courtyard was a short flight of steps below her, at the level of the lowest rooms.

It was a pretty courtyard, paved in stone slabs and furnished with orange trees in pots. Awnings provided shade around the edges. In the centre was a large, rectangular swimming pool, which looked very clean and very blue in the sunlight.

She could see no trace of Laurent, so she tentatively made a few more steps forward. On the opposite side, she now saw, there were a white table and four white-painted wood-slat chairs. Two of the chairs were pushed back, the other two drawn up close to the table, and on the table were all the makings of a salad lunch for two.

For Laurent and his wife? Lucy wondered. His girlfriend? He had come to Mal's bar alone, admittedly, but he had said nothing to confirm that he was alone on the island.

Not that it mattered to her, she reminded herself. Except that if there was a woman in the villa—of less generous proportions than Juana—she might have been able to borrow some dry clothes, and would not have been obliged to prowl around in a damp and revealing yellow bikini.

She crossed to the table. And saw, then, that the glass doors behind it led to the room where Laurent had first taken her.

She went inside. The room was low-ceilinged, as all of the villa appeared to be, white-painted, and plainly but expensively furnished. There was the sofa where she had sat earlier, donkey-brown leather, and a twin opposite it. A low marble table between them, low cupboards along one wall—with a brandy decanter and a discarded glass still on top of one of them— and bright modern oil-paintings on the walls. Very smart, she thought, but not at all homely. There were no books, no records, no framed photographs, nothing that told her anything personal about Laurent.

Anyway, she didn't want to know anything personal about him, she scolded herself. He was a stranger, and from the look of things not a particularly pleasant one. All she wanted to do was to find out why he had ordered Alonzo to keep the boats away, and to make sure he wouldn't do it in future.

A slight noise on the marble floor made her turn swiftly, and she saw that he had come through the doors after her.

She stood there for a moment, just looking at him. He was still wearing only shorts. They looked to be the same pair, but they were dry, so presumably he had changed into similar ones while she was showering. The rest of him seemed very long, and very brown. He was at least six foot three, Lucy thought, but he carried his height elegantly: there was nothing gangling about him. He looked just as good in shorts as he had done fully dressed in Mal's bar. Better, even.

And while she had been staring at him, she realised belatedly, he had been appraising her just as thoroughly. That was an unnerving thought. Not that he could see any more than anyone could who watched her sunning herself or swimming in public, but there was something intimate about being alone with him in his villa, wearing only a bikini.

She tried to think of something to say. Like, thank you for the shower and goodbye. But before she could get the words out, he said, 'I'm sorry, I don't have a hairdryer here. But I could ask Juana if she has one, if you wish.'

Lucy swung back her long, damp mass of hair self-consciously. 'Oh, no. That's not necessary. It'll dry very quickly in the sun.'

'Then we should go out into the sun now. You'll join me for lunch?'

No girlfriend, then; no wife. The second place was for her.

'There's really no need,' she said, trying to suppress the absurd pleasure she felt at the offer. 'I've some sandwiches back in the dinghy.'

'And a fish. I did think of offering to have Juana cook it for you, but...'

'But it's much too small.' Lucy laughed. And Laurent laughed, too. What a nice sound it was. How silly she was being, Lucy thought, casting him as an ogre. There had to be some simple explanation for the way Alonzo had acted; there had to be.

'Perhaps you would have caught three or four, if it hadn't been for your encounter with the *Santa Caterina*.'

Perhaps she would. In a roundabout way, Lucy supposed that it was Laurent's fault that she hadn't. At least that was what he was suggesting, as a way of persuading her to stay.

She hesitated, and he went on, 'Please? I've been lunching alone ever since I arrived, and it will be a pleasure to have company.'

She glanced at her watch. It was just after one o'clock. There was more than enough time to get back to Juan before the passengers arrived for the *San Felipe*'s afternoon trip; there was enough time to lunch with Laurent. It would be so nice to lunch with Laurent.

'If you're sure it's no trouble....'

'None at all. Lunch is all waiting for us.'

He led her outside, and across to the table. The lunch was simple, but beautifully set out, in a style that was more French than Minorcan. There were huge tomatoes chopped and doused in oil and lemon, thin slices of *saucisson* and Parma ham, a dish of black olives, a crisp bowl of lettuce and chicory mixed together, a Camembert and a hunk of local cheese. Lucy suddenly realised that she was more hungry than she had thought.

There was wine, too. Laurent withdrew a bottle from an ice-bucket, and poured them a glass each. He raised his to her.

'To chance encounters.'

Chance had actually had very little to do with it, Lucy thought a trifle guiltily, as she echoed him and took a sip of the wine. After all, she had come across the harbour looking for Alonzo's employer; it was just that she hadn't known then that it was Laurent she was looking for.

She would have to ask him about that. But she could eat first, surely? It would only be polite to eat first, and she didn't want to be rude to him again, not after her ungracious behaviour on the quay. Laurent hadn't known, after all, that she had reason to be apprehensive of Alonzo; he must have found her reaction to his rescue totally incomprehensible.

He did not appear to be bearing any grudges. He was charm personified as he helped her to a large portion of salad. It tasted as good as it had looked.

Finally Lucy sat back in her chair, pleasantly satiated. Laurent reached for the wine-bottle, and made as if to pour her another glass.

Oh, no. That would be her third, on top of the brandy. She had to work that afternoon, and before that she had to ask Laurent some awkward questions.

She set her hand over her glass, and looked cautiously at him. She wasn't sure what she was looking

for: something in his face, perhaps, that would tell
her if he had anything to hide from her.

There was nothing. In daylight the planes of his
face were softer than they had appeared in the shadows
of the bar, but there was something firm and authori-
tative about it, all the same. He would be a decisive
man, Lucy thought; she thought now, as she had
thought before, that he was used to being obeyed. He
wasn't smiling, but the little lines about his mouth
reminded her of his ready smile earlier. There was
nothing cruel in his face. It hinted of a thoughtful
nature, of a sensuous streak, but not of viciousness.
He didn't seem like the kind of man who would order
his henchmen to harass pleasure-boats.

But there was no doubt about it, it was the *Santa
Caterina* that had been driven at the *San Felipe*, and
at the *Blue Boat*. It was Alonzo who had accosted
her in Cala Corb. And, if Laurent didn't know about
Alonzo's direct approach, he certainly knew about the
Santa Caterina, because she had told him of it herself.

He turned, and met her gaze.

'I know what you're thinking,' he said.

'You do?' Lucy murmured faintly.

'You're thinking that I must have known, that
evening when we met in the bar, that it was Alonzo
who had upset the *San Felipe*.'

Lucy considered how to answer this. She hadn't
come to any conclusions when Laurent continued,
'And of course, you are partly right. When you mentioned a white power-boat I did wonder whether it
might have been the *Santa Caterina*, but I had no
reason to be certain of it, and I felt that there was
nothing I could say. Naturally when I returned home

I made enquiries, and when I discovered that Alonzo was responsible for your unpleasant experience I immediately ordered him to be sure that he caused no more disruption to the pleasure-boats.'

Lucy said slowly, 'Do you mean that it was you who originally ordered him...'

'To drive the *Santa Caterina* at the pleasure-boats?' Laurent finished for her. 'Naturally not. Alonzo knew that I was anxious to improve the security here, but I had absolutely no idea that he had chosen such a method of carrying out my instructions. I certainly hadn't intended anything of the kind.'

'So you don't know what happened yesterday?'

'Yesterday?' Laurent frowned. 'But it was on Wednesday that we met. I spoke to Alonzo first thing yesterday morning.'

'Well, whatever you told him, he promptly took the *Santa Caterina* over to Cala Corb.'

Lucy explained, succinctly, how Alonzo had approached her on the quay. Laurent listened in silence. She saw his lips go thin and tight, his eyes narrow.

'But this is outrageous,' he said when she finished. He stood up abruptly, pushing his chair back on the flagstones. 'I cannot apologise to you enough. You must appreciate that Alonzo is a very new member of my staff, and that he came to me with excellent references. Believe me, I had not the remotest idea that he would behave in such a fashion. Let me call him at once, and have him apologise to you himself.'

'No!' Lucy cried, involuntarily.

Laurent had already taken a step away. He froze, and turned back towards her.

'You do not wish that?'

What did she wish? Lucy honestly wasn't sure. Relief at Laurent's very obvious ignorance was mingled in her mind with an acute reluctance to face Alonzo again. 'Really,' she said truthfully, 'I'd much rather not see him.'

'Then I shall speak to him immediately after you leave. And please be assured that there will be absolutely no incidents like this in future.'

'Thank you,' Lucy said. She really should be leaving, she thought. It must be—heavens, it was well past two o'clock. She jumped to her feet. 'Look, I must go now, or I'll be late back to the bay. But thank you for lunch, and . . .'

'It's nothing,' Laurent said. 'Let me show you down to the quay.'

He took hold of her arm as he guided her down the steep steps that led from the courtyard down to the harbourside. It was a reassuring feeling, the touch of his fingers against her bare skin. Lucy couldn't help being aware that Alonzo was somewhere behind them at the villa; she was glad she wasn't going to have to see him again.

'Oh,' said Laurent, as they stepped on to the boards of the quay, 'your fishing-rod. I almost forgot. I had Alonzo retrieve the pieces while you were showering, but I am afraid it is quite beyond repair. Naturally I shall replace it for you. If I bring the replacement over to Cala Corb tomorrow afternoon . . .?'

That was a generous offer. Lucy felt that she perhaps should have refused it. But she really couldn't afford to pay for a new rod herself out of her tiny wages, and she couldn't help thinking that it was Alonzo's fault that the original had been broken.

Anyway, that meant she would see Laurent again the next day and she liked the thought of that.

'That's kind of you,' she said. 'I'm generally at the bay from lunch time until the boat leaves.'

'I shall look forward to seeing you then.'

He reached to pull the *Sophie* closer to the quayside, and held the stern steady as she jumped aboard, then helped her to cast off. She turned back to look at the quay when she was perhaps fifty yards out into the harbour, and saw that he was still standing there, gazing after her.

There was barely time after Lucy reached Cala Corb to get the *San Felipe* ready for its afternoon trip before the first passengers arrived. There certainly wasn't time for her to explain to Juan exactly what she had been doing that morning, and he didn't ask any questions, or mention the missing rod. Lucy's T-shirt was missing, too—she thought she must have left it at Laurent's villa—but she found a spare one in one of the *San Felipe*'s lockers, and slipped that on over her bikini.

She would have to say something about Laurent, she supposed, particularly if he was going to turn up at Cala Corb the next day with her T-shirt and a new rod. But did she have to tell Juan that he had been behind Alonzo's actions? In the end, she decided not to. Juan seemed to have half forgotten the incidents already, and Lucy was satisfied now that they were unlikely to be repeated.

Though that didn't exactly explain, she thought uneasily, why they had happened in the first place. Improving security at the villa, Laurent had said. That was odd. Minorca didn't have a serious crime problem, and she doubted whether villas such as Laurent's were prime targets for thieves, anyway. It was a holiday home, obviously: furnished with good modern furniture, but not with valuable antiques. He wouldn't keep great quantities of money or jewellery there, surely; there couldn't be so very much to steal. A guard dog might have made sense—but an all-out campaign against the boats in the harbour? It just didn't add up.

But it wasn't her problem, she told herself firmly. Laurent wasn't her man. He was a very attractive man, admittedly, but she had told herself all summer that she wasn't interested in holiday romances. And, she added, a little disappointed in spite of her good resolutions, he had given her no reason to think that he was interested in a closer relationship with her.

Saturday was another very hot day. The water in the harbour was still and flat, and the air seemed to cling around Lucy as she wiped down the *San Felipe*. The harbour trip was going to be crowded again: by two o'clock they had sold the last of the tickets. She counted the little plastic cups as she stacked them in the drinks locker, making sure that there would be enough for all the passengers. Every day there were a few less cups—some people broke them, a few idiots tossed them overboard. They needed a new supply. They were on their last bottle of gin, too; Juan would have to visit the distillery the next day, she thought to herself, and collect another load of samples.

Laurent appeared at two-thirty. Lucy had been keeping half an eye open for the *Santa Caterina*, but in fact he didn't come on the boat: he walked down the concrete slipway that led from the road above to the quay, and she didn't see him until he called out to her.

He was wearing white shorts and a short-sleeved shirt striped in blue, and he not only looked handsome, he looked cool and relaxed, which didn't seem fair when he had caught Lucy with sticky hands and a sweaty face. No wonder he hadn't gone overboard for her, she thought ruefully; on the last two occasions when he'd seen her she had been wearing a shapeless green boiler-suit and a soggy T-shirt, and though this time she had had warning of their meeting she could hardly have dressed like a fashion plate to hose down the benches of the *San Felipe*.

She pushed her hair out of her eyes, and made her way to the stern.

'Any chance of selling you a ticket, sir?' she said lightly. 'We're fully booked this afternoon, but there are places going on the mystery tour tomorrow morning.'

Laurent smiled. 'To be honest, I hadn't even thought of it. You're right, though—I really ought to come with you some time. I've seen very little of the island.'

Lucy didn't like to press him, when that sounded so much like a polite brush-off. 'How long have you been here?' she asked instead.

The smile disappeared. Heavens, he was sensitive! It wasn't as if she had plied him with personal questions on either of their previous meetings, but even this tiny hint of friendly curiosity seemed to set him on edge.

'A week or two,' he said vaguely. 'I brought you the new fishing-rod. It's in my car. Do you have somewhere to leave it during the trip?'

'Juan's hut, over there.'

'I'll just go and get it, then.'

'Hold on, I'll come with you.'

'It's OK for you to leave the boat?'

'Juan will watch it. He's over at the Illa Plana.' She gestured to the tables outside the cave bar, where Juan was lounging with a group of his friends. Juan was half watching her; he raised a hand in acknowledgement. She set her foot on the side of the boat, preparing to jump off, and Laurent reached out to take her hand. He didn't release it when she was standing on the quay next to him.

They walked hand in hand up to the road, where he had parked his car: a dark blue Renault, respectable but not imposing. He unlocked it, and brought out the rod. It was better than the one that had been broken, Lucy saw immediately: fine and supple, with a smooth-running inertia reel and brass fittings.

'That's really nice,' she said. 'Juan will be pleased.'

'I'm not an expert on rods, but they told me in the tackle shop that this was a good light one for fishing in the harbour.'

'Should be. Do you fish yourself?'

'I rarely have the time, even when I'm supposed to be on holiday. I bought a couple of rods while I was in Mahon, though. I'll hope to use them before the summer's over.'

Supposed to be on holiday? What an odd way of phrasing it. Though it was true, Lucy thought:

Laurent hardly seemed like a holiday-maker. Compared to most of the people on the island he was tense and over-alert. Perhaps he did some of his work at the villa, she thought. She didn't like to ask him outright. That might explain his need for security. It might explain why she hadn't seen him before the night when they had met at Mal's. A week or two he had been on the island, but she hadn't seen him before then in any of the bars, at the bay in Villa Carlos town, even on the Santa Caterina in the harbour. She would have noticed him in any of those places, no doubt about that.

She thought about suggesting that they go fishing together some time, but decided against it; it might seem pushy, she thought. Instead she said, 'Juan often fishes from the *Sophie*. He'll take you out, if you want company; or he would be able to find a bigger boat to take you if you'd prefer that.'

'Maybe.'

'Come and meet him,' Lucy persisted.

She set off back down to the bay. It was a moment before Laurent followed her. She almost thought that he would get into his car and drive off instead; evidently he didn't particularly want to meet Juan. But he had to, didn't he see that? Whatever his lack of future intentions, he had held her hand walking up the slipway; that alone, by Juan's standards, made an introduction necessary.

They went over to the Illa Plana. Juan stood up as they approached, and his friends pulled over a couple of chairs for them.

'Glad to meet you, Señor...' Juan began.

'Laurent,' Laurent said firmly. 'And may I call you Juan? Lucy has told me all about you, and about the *San Felipe*.'

And Laurent, thought Lucy, had carefully omitted to give a surname. He had done that at Mal's, too.

Juan looked over the rod professionally, and nodded his approval. He and Laurent discussed fishing for a few minutes. Laurent did know quite a bit about it, however ignorant he had made himself out to be earlier. And he did speak some Catalan. He also bought beers for all Juan's friends. Juan gave Lucy a meaningful look while Laurent was doing this, as if to say that it didn't sway his judgement, but his judgement was favourable anyway.

He probably wouldn't be so approving, Lucy thought, if he realised she had gone alone to Laurent's villa. She had been careful not to make it clear to Juan and Sophie where the accident with the fishing-rod had happened. And she hadn't mentioned the missing T-shirt at all. It was just as well that he hadn't produced it in front of Juan.

As soon as Laurent had downed his beer she stood up, announcing that she must put the rod away and get back to the *San Felipe*. The first customers were starting to congregate on the quayside.

Laurent followed her over to Juan's hut. She stacked the new rod among Juan's collection of bigger and heavier rods.

'I forgot your T-shirt,' Laurent said.

'That's OK. I've got lots.'

'Juana washed and ironed it, but I left it at the villa. I'll bring it over next time.'

Next time, Lucy thought. She turned to look at him. He was standing very close to her, in the tiny patch of shade cast by the wooden door of the hut. She could smell the faint piney scent he gave off. His eyes looked very dark, even black in the shadow.

'Do you work in the evenings?' he asked.

She shook her head. 'Only the afternoons, generally. Sometimes I babysit for Juan and Sophie—that's his wife, my aunt. I go to the bars in Villa Carlos, now and then to the discos, see friends in Mahon. I'm pretty busy.'

'You're busy tonight?'

Tonight! What had she been saying? Burbling on about all the things she did in the evenings, like a nervous schoolkid, when all the time he'd been thinking of asking her out. And when she wanted—oh, holiday romance or not, mystery or not, she wanted to go out with him all right.

'I haven't made any plans for tonight.'

'Could I pick you up at about eight, then?'

Lucy thought, suddenly, does he mean this as a recompense for yesterday? Does he think he ought to ask me out, to make up for Alonzo's upsetting me? She looked into his eyes again. It was like touching a live wire, and receiving a small electric shock: a current seemed to run through her. He was so close. She only had to reach out a hand, and she could touch him...

'Fine,' she murmured.

Laurent gave a slow smile. 'You'd better tell me where to find you.'

'Oh, yes. Do you know Villa Carlos at all?'

She explained to him where Juan and Sophie's villa was.

'I'll find it,' Laurent assured her. 'Look, hadn't you better be getting back to the boat?'

Lucy glanced past him. Juan was already on the boat, she saw, and embarking the passengers. 'Heavens, I had!' she exclaimed.

'I'll see you later.' He moved a step forward, and set his hands on her shoulders. His lips just brushed her forehead. Then he was striding away, and Lucy was gazing dizzily at the crowded quayside, and at the passengers queueing up by the notice for the harbour tour.

CHAPTER FOUR

'LAURENT,' Sophie said thoughtfully, as she posted another spoonful of apple purée into baby Cara. 'He's French, then?'

'I guess so. But he speaks very good English.'

'Guess? Didn't you ask him?'

Lucy flushed. 'He's not an easy person to ask questions of.'

'Well, that can hardly be a state secret. I'll ask him myself, if you won't.'

'Oh, I will,' Lucy said hastily.

Sophie picked up a cloth, and mopped Cara's chin. 'What do you know about him?' she asked.

'Not a lot. He's in his early thirties, I should think. He's a banker, on holiday here for the summer. He's got a villa over on the other side of Mahon harbour.'

'On holiday for the summer?' Sophie echoed.

'A few weeks.'

'Few weeks? Bankers aren't generally renowned for the long holidays they take.'

'I think he's doing some work while he's here,' Lucy said lamely.

Sophie abandoned Cara for a moment, and turned her full attention on to Lucy. 'You honestly don't know anything about him, do you?'

'Well, I only just met him!' Lucy said defensively.

'Is he married, for instance?'

'Of course not!' Sophie's cool look didn't waver. 'He wouldn't have asked me out otherwise, would he?' Lucy retorted.

'Ask him,' Sophie said. 'Look, Lu, I know some of the English girls on holiday here get up to all sorts of capers, but you're not on holiday. You're with me and Juan, right? And I know you wouldn't take it kindly if Juan demanded that you have a chaperon, but you do have to think about us, and about how the things you do look to the people we know.'

Lucy sighed. 'I'll give you a full report in the morning, Sophie.'

'I'll look forward to it.' Sophie said it severely, but then she gave Lucy a broad smile. 'I really am glad, you know, Lu, that you've found someone. I wouldn't want to see you mope over Hugh for ever. But it's just that you have to be careful, particularly on a holiday island like this.'

'I will,' Lucy assured her. She drained her cup of coffee, and went up to her room to change.

Actually, she thought, as she was combing her hair through before pinning it up, she wasn't moping over Hugh at all. She had hardly thought about Hugh all summer. It was nearly a year since he had broken their engagement, and even then it hadn't come as a shock: Lucy had known that they had been growing apart ever since she had left home to go off to university. It was just that she hadn't met anyone since who had particularly attracted her.

Laurent attracted her, all right. But at the same time, this was the holiday romance she had sworn to avoid. Holiday romances with the wrong man were just plain sordid, she and Vanessa had agreed over a bottle of wine, weeks before; holiday romances with the right man led to far too much heartbreak. Therefore, no holiday romances.

Maybe it wouldn't be just a holiday romance, though. She would have to find out some more about him tonight, if only to appease Sophie and Juan, and maybe it would turn out that there was a chance of a long-term future for their relationship. She didn't know yet where Laurent lived, even. It might not even be France. And if it was—hadn't she thought of working in Paris herself, once she left the university?

Lucy, Lucy, she scolded herself. You're getting carried away. One date, that's all he's offered you. Enjoy it for itself. Keep your heart safely to yourself, and concentrate on getting to the bottom of this little mystery about Alonzo. Playing detective will be much more fun than falling in love.

There was a gentle knock on the door. Not Laurent already! Luckily it was only little Maria, curious about Lucy's preparations. Lucy set her to work handing over the pins she needed to fasten up her hair.

By the time Laurent really did knock on the front door, she was almost ready. White trousers and a loose green silky top, white high-heeled sandals, her hair in a neat pleat, and just a touch of make-up. Was that the kind of look Laurent liked? she wondered, as she sprayed herself generously with the Arpège Sophie had lent her in an attempt to make up for the earlier inquisition. She didn't yet know even that.

When she got downstairs she found Laurent in the front room, holding Cara in a surprisingly professional manner, and laughingly fending off the other children. He was wearing fawn trousers and a cream shirt, open at the neck, smart and undemonstrative like all the clothes Lucy had seen him in. He returned the baby to Sophie, ruffled Manuel's hair, and came to take Lucy's arm.

'Back before midnight,' Juan said gruffly, from his armchair in front of the television.

'I promise, Juan.' Lucy loosed her arm for long enough to give the children their goodnight kisses, and followed Laurent down the path to his car.

'Nice kids,' he said, as they were settling into the Renault.

'. . . shame about the mess,' Lucy added, laughing at his expression.

'I did wonder if it was a family trait . . .'

'Oh, no, just Sophie. My mother's ever so tidy.'

They talked about Lucy's family for the rest of the journey through Villa Carlos. Laurent drove straight through the town, taking the coast road that led to Mahon.

'We're going into Mahon?' Lucy asked.

'If that's all right with you. I wasn't sure about taking you to a restaurant in Villa Carlos.'

'I'm not exactly a regular in most of them. I think I've had two pizzas and one paella at restaurants there all summer,' Lucy said with a laugh. 'And as for Mahon, just about anywhere there will be new to me.'

'I've booked a table at a fish place, but we can look around if you'd prefer something different.'

'Sounds fine.'

It was fine, particularly as the restaurateur showed them to his best table, at the edge of a terrace overlooking the harbour. It was a fine, clear evening, and the sun was only just setting over the hills. All round the harbour, the lights of the villas and yachts shone out at them. A fishing-boat drifted past, just far enough away for its engine to be inaudible; on the pavement below the promenaders of Mahon wandered and chattered in the glow of the bright light from of the bars.

'Lovely harbour, isn't it?' Laurent murmured.

'It's a lovely island. You're very lucky to live here.'

'I'm lucky to be here,' Laurent agreed. 'But I'd never wish to live here all the year round, I'm afraid. I'm a big-city man at heart, I get to miss the bustle after a short while.'

'Paris? Or London?'

'Paris.'

'I'm a Londoner. That's real life, isn't it? The grey skies, the rain, and two weeks in the sun to look forward to every summer. Sophie thinks the rest of the family are mad not to have followed her out here, but I wouldn't want to be here permanently, either. I'm like you, I love the big-city buzz too much to turn my back on it for ever.'

A waiter appeared just then, with a wine-bucket.

'Heavens, that's quick service!' Lucy exclaimed. The restaurant was crowded, and Minorcan service was generally friendly but on the slow side, so she had expected a much longer wait.

Laurent laughed at her surprise. 'I've never been here before,' he explained, 'but I asked my neighbour where I should take you, and he recommended this place. He's a friend of the proprietor, and he must have asked him to look after us specially.'

'Your neighbour? That's the nightclub owner?'

A hint of a frown crossed Laurent's face. 'How on earth did you know that?'

To Lucy's annoyance, she felt herself blushing. No need for embarrassment, she reminded herself, it wasn't as if she had been prying into Laurent's life personally when she had found out about the nightclub owner. She hadn't known then that Alonzo was anything to do with him.

She hadn't meant to raise the subject of Alonzo yet. Laurent had just started to open up, she sensed; she had wanted to find out much more about him before moving on to sensitive territory. Oh, well, too late. She told him briefly about how she had checked with Anna, and how the other boat guide had told her who lived in the villas that used the long wooden quay.

Laurent's frown was still there, drawing a couple of vertical lines above his brows. Lucy didn't like it. There was nothing sinister in what she had done, surely; nothing strange in what she'd discovered. She tried to change the subject.

'Your other neighbour is Carmen Torres, Anna told me. You know, the singer? Have you met her at all?'

Laurent barely seemed to hear her. He said, in a low, intense voice, 'So the boat guides tell their passengers all about the inhabitants of the villas?'

Lucy shrugged. 'Not all about them. If you came on the boat trip you'd find out. Well, not from the *San Felipe* you wouldn't, because I don't really say anything myself about the villa people. Anna knows most of the residents much better than I do, of course, and so do many of the other guides from Cales Fons and Mahon. But they certainly don't mention

everyone—just a few people the English tourists might
have heard of. You know the tourists are almost all
English round here. Most of them haven't even heard
of Carmen Torres. And there's no reason for any of
the guides to mention you. You're not famous, are
you?'

She watched Laurent's face carefully throughout
this long speech. He wasn't famous, was he? she
thought. He was as good-looking as many actors, but
somehow he didn't *look* famous. The few actors and
television celebrities she had met had all seemed very
conscious of the image they projected, of the fact that
they were being watched all the time. Laurent had
none of their peculiar brand of self-satisfaction. But
there was something strange in his manner, an odd
mixture of basic self-assurance mixed with a sort of
edgy nervousness. It was almost as if he *did* feel that
he was being watched, but that he wasn't used to it,
as a celebrity would have been.

He didn't answer her question directly. Instead he
said, 'Did Anna tell you anything about me?'

'A little, yes. Of course she knows much more than
she puts into her commentaries; she told me a bit
about all the villa owners who use the same quay as
you do. She thought you had bought the villa quite
recently, and that you were a French banker. Which
is true, isn't it?' It struck her now that, though she
had repeated Anna's information to Juan and Sophie,
she had not actually had any other confirmation of
Laurent's job. Maybe he wasn't really a banker.
Maybe he did something else, something that caused
him to need to keep his whereabouts private?

Her earlier distrust of him came flooding back. She shouldn't have agreed to come out with him, she thought; she shouldn't be playing detective. Juan was right, it could gain nothing, and it might even be dangerous. Alonzo *was* dangerous, she could swear it. That scene at Cala Corb had been positively threatening, and it had surely been deliberate, too, when he had rocked the *Sophie* and sent her flying overboard.

Maybe Laurent himself wasn't dangerous—at least, not in the same way—but he wasn't being open. He wasn't telling her anything, he was just questioning her all the time!

'More or less,' he said offhandedly. He was still abstracted, still frowning. But there was nothing upsetting in what she had told him, Lucy thought; it had to be his own secrets that were disturbing him.

The waiter came up to take their order, but Laurent waved him away again. He leaned forward, setting his elbows on the table. His eyes were looking for hers, but Lucy tried to avoid their gaze.

'So if anyone were to come and ask Anna about—about, say, my neighbour who runs a nightclub—she would know which villa he lived in?'

What on earth was he getting at? Lucy shifted edgily. 'She'd know, of course. Minorca's a small place, Laurent. There are less inhabitants on the whole island than in any fair-sized city in England or France. Mahon is a small town. People are friendly and curious here, they gossip, and it's Anna's job to know about interesting happenings and interesting people. This isn't an island for recluses. Everybody knows everybody else. That's not just true of Anna; people like Mal and Vanessa know just as much as she does, if not more. But any of them would be suspicious if a stranger started asking questions. Not that there's much to fear on the island—the crime-rate is low here. I haven't heard of any serious burglaries in or around Mahon all summer.'

Laurent didn't reply. He sat in silence, apparently thinking over what she had said. Then he seemed to recollect himself, and brighten up. 'I'm sorry,' he said. 'I didn't mean to alarm you. Have you had a chance to look at the menu? Or shall we ask the waiter what he recommends today?'

And that was it, Lucy thought. She wasn't going to get any explanations, any confidences, just a blithe apology for unnerving her. And then a barrelful of superficial charm, doubtless, to wash her doubts away as thoroughly as he had done over lunch at the villa. Except that this time her doubts had taken even deeper root. He wouldn't be able to wipe them away again, not until he gave her a proper explanation.

He wouldn't bother to do that, clearly. And why should he? She was no more than a passing acquaintance to him, she supposed. It wasn't even a real holiday romance. She hadn't had any compliments from him, or any kisses. He had dutifully entertained her after her ducking at the villa, and had asked her out once to dinner. Big deal!

So she would treat him just as superficially as he treated her, and concentrate on the dinner. At least that was a treat: she couldn't afford harbourside fish restaurants herself, and nor could most of Vanessa's friends. She buried herself in the menu.

So did Laurent. Once they had ordered, he steered the conversation around to impersonal subjects. They talked about the restaurants of Ciudadela, the town on the other side of the island. They talked about the archaeological remains on the island, and discussed which were the best bays for underwater swimming.

Laurent was charming, no doubt about it, Lucy reluctantly conceded. He didn't pretend to know Minorca well himself, but he seemed genuinely interested in everything she told him about the island. He was really knowledgeable about ancient history, and was able to explain the purpose of some of the stone monuments that until then had been no more than mysteries to her. And, though he played down his expertise, it wasn't difficult to tell that he was a very experienced swimmer and diver. And he was so damned attractive. She kept finding her gaze lingering on his long, elegant hands, the fine lines of his face, the way his short, dark hair curled over his ears. Every time she caught herself doing it, she gave herself a mental scolding, and tried to redouble her concentration on their conversation.

They ate gazpacho, cold tomato soup, followed by the swordfish the waiter recommended. Both were excellent. And now there was just an ice-cream to follow, and he would be taking her home. Relieved, probably, that she hadn't learned anything she wasn't supposed to learn.

Sophie wouldn't be relieved at that, though. Sophie would think the worst, if Lucy returned without even discovering whether Laurent really was French. Whether he really was married. Of course he wasn't, she told herself, glancing at his ringless left hand. Then she remembered the ease with which he had handled baby Cara, and knew she would need a much fuller account of his past if she was to satisfy Sophie.

Not that she would be seeing him again. But still, she didn't want Sophie to think ...

'Nice?' Laurent asked.

Lucy glanced across the table at him. Oh, the ice-cream. 'Yes, delicious,' she said. 'It's like eating cold chocolate truffles. I've been looking at the ice-cream adverts ever since I arrived on Minorca, and daring myself to try one of these specials.'

'Why not? You're slim, you can afford to indulge yourself sometimes.' Laurent gave her a teasing smile.

'Not too often.' Lucy hesitated. Now or never, she thought. 'You eat out a lot, do you, in Paris?'

'Most Parisians do. They don't go in for entertaining at home as much as the English: life revolves around cafés and restaurants. I have a lot of business lunches, and I dine out quite often, too. I'm very fond of good *haute cuisine*. Alas, there's nothing on Minorca to rival the best Paris restaurants.'

That was a little unfair to the swordfish, Lucy thought, but she supposed it had been simple stuff, compared to what he was used to in Paris.

'And does your wife cook well?'

'My wife?' His elegant façade fell for a moment, and Lucy glimpsed something much more raw beneath it. For a moment, she was sorry she had asked.

He recovered quickly. 'Actually,' he said smoothly, 'my wife was an excellent cook. I particularly miss her omelettes. We were divorced almost a year ago.'

'I'm sorry. Her choice or yours?'

He was on guard now; he didn't react. 'Hers,' he said lightly, 'but largely my fault, I fear. I tend to work very long hours, and Catherine felt she was being neglected.'

'Did she work?'

'Not outside the home, no. We have a son—Gilles is six now.'

Manuel's age, Lucy thought. No wonder Laurent had seemed at home with Sophie's family.

'Perhaps,' she said, 'you would have been better suited to a career woman.'

'Perhaps so,' he agreed. 'But it is too late now. I do not intend to marry again. And you? Is there a boyfriend back in England?'

Subject dismissed. At least she had had an answer of sorts, but she clearly wasn't going to be told any more. And he wasn't really interested in her love-life, Lucy thought, annoyed; it was just the first way that came to hand of changing the subject. She didn't tell him about Hugh. Instead she described a couple of her university friends, acquaintances rather than real boyfriends, about whom she could talk jokingly with no fear of giving away anything important. Laurent teased her in return, but lightly, and soon they had changed the subject again.

They lingered over their coffees. It was pleasant sitting on the terrace, poised between the bright lights of the restaurant and the darkness of the harbour. It was pleasant sitting opposite Laurent. His charm might be a façade, but it was a very nice façade, Lucy thought dreamily. She wouldn't see him again, but she might as well let this evening last as long as possible.

Laurent seemed to think the same. On the pavement outside the restaurant, he hesitated.

'We could go to a nightclub...'

A nightclub. That would mean dancing with him. That would mean feeling his strong arms around her, and smelling that piney smell of his, and looking into his eyes. That would...no, that wouldn't do at all.

'I'm not really a nightclub person. And I promised Juan I'd be back by midnight, while the nightclubs don't really get going much earlier than that.'

'A bar, then? We could go to Cales Fons, or to somewhere in Mahon if you prefer? Or even to Mal's?'

To Mal's. If ever she was to catch him off guard again, Lucy thought, it would be far more likely to be in Mal's than in any crowded Mahon discotheque.

'Mal's would be fine. Mal's would be best, really. The Cales Fons bars are all noisy, but Cala Corb's always quiet, even when every table's taken at Mal's. Have you heard Pedro play? Mal sing?'

'I came back to hear Pedro on the evening I met you there. I didn't realise that Mal sang as well.'

'Late at night, usually. But we might be able to persuade him to sing early if he's in the right mood.'

They drove back to Villa Carlos in silence. Lucy found herself thinking about Catherine. Imagine being married to Laurent, and then losing him. No, not merely losing him, choosing to go. Had Catherine found out his guilty secret? Or had she been imagining it all? Was there no guilty secret? Had there been no more to his divorce than Laurent had said, that he had neglected his wife for a long time, and finally paid the price?

Was Catherine blonde? she wondered. Was Catherine pretty? Oh, stop it, Lucy. You can't be jealous, not of the ex-wife of a man you're not going to see again.

She glanced at Laurent's clear-cut, handsome profile, as he stared ahead at the darkening road, and thought, oh, if only he had no secret. If only he were everything he seems to be, and no more. If only, if only . . .

He pulled up the car in one of the quiet side streets above Cala Corb, and came round to let Lucy out and take her arm. A sudden impulse led her to lead him, not to the broad concrete slope that led down to the bay, but along the road that led up, to the narrow open space called the Miranda Cala Corb.

They stopped there, by the fence that cut off the sheer drop down. The bay was a long way below. On the clifftop at the other side, the lights of the Don Carlos hotel shone bright against the dark sky. A couple of boats were moving way out in the main harbour; a yellow moon hung over the hills. Odd snatches of guitar music reached them, drifting up from the bars down by the quayside.

Laurent moved closer, and slipped an arm around Lucy's waist. She could feel his fingers, warm through the thin fabric of her silky top. His shoulder was at just the right height for her to rest her head against. A tempting thought.

They had been fencing with each other all evening, Lucy reminded herself. And now, if they were acting like lovers, it was no more than an illusion. What did she really know about him, even now? Barely enough to satisfy Sophie; not nearly enough to satisfy her.

The guitarists at the Illa Plana finished their song, and a scatter of clapping stole through the darkness. Laurent drew his arm away.

'Which way?'

'Here. Mind the steps, they're steep in places, and you don't know them like I do.'

She had to take his hand, because the steps were badly lit as well as steep. When they reached the bottom Laurent held her back, gently. They stood there in the inky shadows. The light and bustle of the bars was only a few yards away, and yet it seemed like a different world.

'We can't walk round this side of the bay?' Laurent asked.

'No. On the other side we can go out to the point, and a little way past it. There may be someone fishing out there.'

'You don't mind walking in the dark?'

It was just what she did want to do, Lucy thought suddenly. She didn't want to go into Mal's, and have Mal eye her and Laurent, and wonder how things were between them. She didn't want to leave him yet. She wanted to be with him, in the dark, enjoying the illusion. She pulled his hand gently in the direction of the path.

They skirted round close to the water past the *San Felipe* at its mooring, past Mal's, past the Illa Plana with its little group of guitarists. A little further along, the concrete path gave way to rock.

There was a dim light, shining from half-way up the steps that led to the Don Carlos. Then they rounded the point, and were in darkness.

There was a fisherman; he was fishing from the rocks on the very tip of the point. The moon barely lit the end of his rod; he had a torch by his bucket, shining away from the water, to keep any passers-by from trampling his tackle and bait. They moved on past him. There the cliff curved back a little, making a shallow depression that was out of sight of both the bay and the hotel on the clifftop. The rock cut off the noise of the bars. The only sound was the light lapping of the water on the rocks at the harbour's edge.

Laurent loosed Lucy's hand, and moved forwards almost to the water's edge. Lucy took a step backwards. It brought her right against the smooth rock surface of the cliff. She leaned back against the rock, and watched Laurent. She could see the outline of him clearly, tall and slim and straight, silhouetted against the faint light of the moon. His villa was almost opposite, she thought.

She saw him turn towards her. He moved slowly, into the shadows where she stood. He kept moving until he was almost touching her. Then his hands came out and took her shoulders, and he drew her gently towards him.

For a moment that felt like an eternity, there was nothing but the sound of his breathing, loud against the silence. Then his mouth came down, and found hers.

Instinctively, unconsciously, her arms moved round his neck and her body urged itself forward until it collided with his. Her mouth opened under the gentle but insistent pressure; his hands slid down her back, and rested on the curve of her hips. The barriers that had divided them all evening seemed to have been melted by the moonlight. It felt like a first fulfilment of an unspoken promise that had been made the first moment they had seen each other in Mal's empty bar.

A moment later, Laurent drew away. His mouth abandoned hers, his hands deserted her body. Lucy swayed backwards. The cliff, cold and unyielding, caught her.

'We'd best be getting to the bar,' Laurent said, 'if you want a drink before I drop you back at midnight. Careful on the rocks, they look slippery to me.'

His voice was low and even-toned, impersonal. It seemed as if, without a word or a look, he was denying the sensations that they had just shared. What sensations? Lucy scolded herself. Pure chemistry, physical attraction, that was all. And that from a man she didn't trust an inch and didn't expect to see ever again.

'They're quite dry,' she said sharply, and moved to follow him.

In fact it was tricky negotiating the uneven surface in her high-heeled sandals, but she would rather have slipped than taken his hand. They arrived at Mal's without incident. The light above the tables seemed painfully fierce. The tables were crowded with tourists. The Manchester flight and the Luton flight, Lucy thought, as she hurried past them and into the dimness of the cave.

Was her hair mussed? Her lipstick smudged? If it was, Mal made no comment, and mercifully there was nobody else she recognised in the bar. A couple of stools by the counter were empty. Lucy slipped gratefully on to one of them.

Mal was busy serving. He gave Lucy a nod of acknowledgement, and she nodded back, to reassure him that they would wait their turn. A dozen tourists later, he came across.

'Brandy?' Laurent asked Lucy.

That was what she had drunk at his villa. 'No, wine,' she responded.

He ordered one cognac and one glass of wine without comment. And said to Mal, 'We were hoping that we could persuade you to sing.'

'I always do, darlings. Around one o'clock.'

'Lucy's Cinderella tonight. I promised to get her home at midnight.'

Mal's bushy eyebrows lifted a little. 'I'll consider it,' he said with a half-smile.

Laurent raised his glass to Lucy's. A toast to what? she wondered. The kiss? Heavens, it had only been a kiss. Dozens of men had kissed her. Surely he hadn't realised what an extraordinary effect that kiss had had on her. Her limbs had seemed to turn to liquid, and his every touch had boiled along her veins. An entirely irrational physical response. She didn't even trust him.

He smiled, and his eyes sought hers. They found hers. It was a very intimate look. What an even shade of brown his eyes were, like velvet. The skin at the corners crinkled a little as he smiled.

'You would make a better Cinderella,' he murmured, 'with your hair loose.'

'Would I?'

He set his glass on the counter, and reached out to pull out one of the pins. And another, and another. Lucy sat there, unmoving, until every hairpin was gone and her long, blonde hair fell in dishevelled waves around her shoulders.

'That's better,' Laurent said critically. He combed his fingers slowly through it.

'I thought you'd like it done up.'

He shook his head. 'Next time, leave it like that.'

Next time? But there wouldn't be a next time, Lucy thought. How could there be, when he wasn't being honest or open with her?

The sharp twang of a guitar tore her attention away from him. It was Mal. He had called Pedro from the forecourt back into the bar, and was getting ready to sing.

CHAPTER FIVE

TUESDAY, early afternoon. Hot. Lucy had put on a yellow beach suit, shorts and suntop, and had found an old straw sunhat to cover her head.

She drove the moped she had hired for the day slowly across the bumpy roads of Villa Carlos, and coasted down the slope that led to Cala Corb. Juan and Sophie were both pottering on the *San Felipe*. The children went to visit Juan's parents in the inland village of Alayor on Tuesday afternoons, and Sophie did the commentaries for Juan while Lucy was allowed the afternoon off.

Sophie looked up at the sound of the moped clattering over the concrete, and drifted lazily to the stern of the boat.

'Tickets going well?' Lucy asked.

'All sold,' Sophie replied. 'Hot day, tourists flying back tomorrow, you know. Vanessa sold the lot, we haven't even had the sign out down here.'

'You should do that,' Lucy half protested. 'We've still to sell the tickets for tomorrow.'

'They'll go. Oh, Vanessa was looking for you, Lucy. Some friends of hers are going over to Palma for a few days on the ferry. They can find you a floor, she says, if you want to come.'

'But the boat...'

'The boat won't sink while you're away.'

Lucy grinned. What a typical Sophie remark that was. Work always came second in Sophie's life; problems were left to cure themselves, or tackled when they turned into urgent crises. And under the easy-going surface, a shrewd and generous mind was always working away. Sophie had seen that Lucy was feeling low, and was looking for a way to cheer her up.

'I'll think about it,' she said.

'You'll be back for supper?'

'Round six, I reckon. Probably before you're back yourself.'

'Likely to have caught enough fish to cook?'

'I doubt it.'

'See you, then. Have fun.'

'Have a good trip.'

Lucy restarted the moped engine, roared over to Juan's hut, leaned the bike against the wooden side of it, and went to rummage inside for her fishing tackle.

She was planning to ride up to Fornells, a village on the northern coast of the island which was rapidly expanding into a centre for holiday-makers and water sports. She picked a collapsible rod, strapped it carefully to the side of the moped, checked once again that the bag on the back contained everything she would need, and set off with a wave to Juan and Sophie.

Palma, she thought, as she chugged through Villa Carlos. Maybe she should go. Anything to get away from Mahon harbour. Even Fornells wasn't far enough away. Palma would be much better.

It didn't seem fair to Sophie and Juan, though, to act as if her heart was broken when the whole thing

had been so trivial. A man had asked her out once
and kissed her once. She had kept on telling herself
that she didn't even trust him, but here she was more
downcast at his failure to contact her again than she
had been when Hugh had jilted her. Idiotic, that was
what it was. Utterly foolish of her.

She hadn't even mentioned Laurent to Vanessa. She
had done her best to be gay and cheerful all through
the previous week but obviously it wasn't fooling
Sophie. It wasn't fooling her, either. However much
she smiled, there was still an annoying ache somewhere in the region of her heart. However often she
told herself that she wouldn't, she still glanced up at
his villa every time the *San Felipe* passed the wooden
quay on the far side of Mahon harbour. She hadn't
had so much as a glimpse of him. She wasn't even
sure that he was still on the island.

Silly, silly girl. Forget him, she told herself. No
holiday romances—that was what you wanted, wasn't
it? Enjoy the rest of the summer on your own.

She rode slowly through Mahon, and along the road
that led inland towards Alayor. Along the roadside
the prickly pears were in bloom; on the walls and roofs
of the cottages big yellow melons had been laid out
to ripen in the sun.

In the centre of the island, the road began to climb,
skirting round Monte Toro, the tallest mountain on
Minorca, with an old monastery at its summit. Lucy
stopped by the roadside and had a drink of orange
before urging the little moped onwards towards the
sea.

She rode through pine forests, and then emerged
above Cala Blanca, the head of the great bay on which

Fornells stood. The last stretch of the journey was a pleasure, downhill with plenty of shade, and occasional glimpses of the sea to spur her onwards.

Fornells was busy. Though it was siesta time by Minorcan standards, some tourists were still finishing lunch in the cafés along the waterside, and others were prowling around the narrow whitewashed streets of the old fishing village. In the bay, a few flashes of colour marked the location of windsurfers. Lucy parked her moped by the harbour breakwater, wandered along to the end of it, set up her rod, and settled down to doze in the sun. She wasn't really concerned about catching fish: the rod was just an excuse, she half-admitted to herself, for not bringing any of her course work with her.

It was hot in the afternoon sunshine, and the breakwater sheltered her from the wind that blew across the bay. After a while, Lucy fell asleep.

She woke again slowly, and glanced around her. Her rod was still propped up where she had left it, the line reaching down into the water of the harbour, but her bait, she knew, would have been taken long before. The sun had moved round a long way. She glanced at her watch. Heavens, it was almost half-past five, and she had told Sophie she'd be back for supper around six. She hurriedly packed up and made her way back to the moped.

She was nearing the top of the hill above Cala Blanca when the engine began to make some thumping and spluttering noises. Lucy groaned to herself. She stopped for a moment, then tried to restart the engine. This time it refused to catch at all.

It took her another ten minutes of vain attempts to start the moped, interspersed with greasy fumblings around the little engine, to cotton on to the awful reality. She had run out of petrol. And on Minorca, the very last place for anyone to even cut it fine on petrol, because everyone on the island knew how sparsely provided it was with filling stations.

She thought. There was a garage in Alayor, she was almost certain. That was a good five miles from where she was, and she couldn't think of another one any nearer. She got back on the moped, set her feet on the pedals, and started to pump away.

By the time the houses of Alayor came into sight she was sweating and puffing. And it was a quarter to seven, with another longish journey still to come once she had filled up with petrol. She would miss supper for certain. Perhaps, she thought, she would be able to beg a meal off Señor and Señora Ribero, Juan's parents.

Señora Ribero was out when she arrived at their little house—returning Manuel, Maria and Cara to their parents. Señor Ribero insisted that Lucy wait for her. She drank a great deal of coffee. Then Señora Ribero reappeared and began to prepare a large meal of lamb chops and aubergines. It was delicious, but it wasn't ready to eat until past nine o'clock. So it was nearly ten before Lucy found herself waving goodbye and setting out again on the road to Mahon.

No problem. Sophie and Juan weren't the types to worry. If they'd had a telephone she could have warned them how late she would be, but they didn't, so that was that. They surely wouldn't agonise about her fate until midnight at the very earliest.

She was right there. When she reached the villa at just past half-past ten, Sophie and Juan were watching a quiz show on television.

'Sorry I missed supper,' Lucy said. She sat down in the living-room, and in the intervals between the questions on television she explained why she was late.

Juan grunted. 'Exercise probably did you good.'

'Don't tell me,' groaned Sophie, 'that's a dig at me!' She looked down and surveyed the hips that had spread after Cara's birth, and that she had not yet managed to slim down again. 'Pity it happened tonight, though. Mind, it's all my fault.'

'What's all your fault?'

'You missing your boyfriend. I had a note for you this morning, delivered to the *San Felipe*, but I clean forgot to hand it over when you came down to the harbour.'

'My boyfriend!'

'Laurent. He came round to call for you earlier this evening, but of course you weren't here.'

Lucy stared. Laurent had written her a note? He had called round? She had missed him? How could Sophie be so casual about it?

'Have you still got the note?'

'It's somewhere here.' Sophie stood up, and began to dig around her pockets. Finally she unearthed a plain white envelope, rather grubby, and handed it over.

'Lucy, *San Felipe*' was written on it in firm, neat handwriting. Lucy ripped it open.

The note inside was very short. 'Dear Lucy,' it said, 'can you manage supper tonight? I'll call for you about eight-thirty? Ring me before six if you can't make it. Laurent.' His phone number was printed on the top right-hand corner.

'I did tell him it was all my fault,' Sophie said. 'Mind, we expected you back any minute, so he waited here for an hour or so. But by then we'd no idea where you'd got to, so he gave up. I said I was awfully sorry.' She gave an apologetic smile. 'Did Señora Ribero give you supper?'

'Did he say anything before he went?'

'Not much. I suppose he was disappointed, but he was very charming about it.'

Lucy got to her feet. 'I'll be back in ten minutes,' she said.

'Where are you going?'

'Just to use the phone.'

There was a call box just down the road, and she rang his number from there. The ringing tone went on and on, but nobody came to answer it. Finally Lucy put the phone down, and walked home in the darkness.

She spent a sleepless night. At least he had wanted to see her. But had he been going to explain everything to her? Was there anything to explain, or had she been an idiot from the start in suspecting him?

At least he wanted to see her. *Had* wanted to see her. Of course he would have been charming to Sophie, but really he had probably been mad when she hadn't turned up. Maybe he wouldn't try again. He couldn't be that keen on her if he had waited ten days before contacting her again. Perhaps it had been a casual impulse, or another girlfriend letting him down. Oh, no, not another girlfriend.

She got up very early in the morning, and played with Maria and Cara until the clock reached the reasonably civilised hour of nine-thirty. Then she made for the door.

'Lucy!'

Sophie's voice caught her in the hall. 'Where are you going?' Sophie asked, emerging out of the kitchen.

'Just down to Cala Corb.'

'You going to phone him again?'

'No.'

'Good.' Sophie grinned. 'I know it matters a lot to you, love, but he'll find a way to see you again if he wants to, honestly. It won't make him any keener if you throw yourself at him.'

'Thanks for the lecture.'

'Well, listen to it, then.' Sophie smiled again, and disappeared.

Lucy went down to Cala Corb. She took out the *Sophie*. She steered the little dinghy straight across Mahon harbour, and drew her up by the long wooden quay. The *Santa Caterina* was moored there. Good, he was likely to be at the villa.

Was he likely to welcome her coming over? Maybe not, she thought uneasily, but she couldn't face the thought of waiting for days to see if he contacted her again. At least this way she would get a quick reaction out of him, and learn if there was any hope for their relationship in future.

She glanced down. She had put on a white blouse and a cotton skirt with a bright pink flower print— pretty, without looking as if she was trying too hard. Alas, it had picked up a dirty mark from the bench in the *Sophie*. She rubbed at it, but without making any visible improvement.

She called out 'hello', in case he was on the terrace half-way up the hillside, where he had been when she last sailed over in the *Sophie*. There was no answer, so she set off up the steps.

She passed the terrace, a neat square of concrete flags with a wrought-iron table and chairs. It bore no sign of recent occupation. She reached the villa. The main courtyard too was deserted.

'Hello!' she called out, slightly louder this time; she didn't want to go into the house without warning him. No reply. She made her way round the edge of the buildings, and came to a smaller yard that was clearly Juana's territory: pots of herbs in the sun, what looked like the villa's kitchen to one side, and opposite, a low, separate building with a washing line suspended from its eaves that might be Juana's and Alonzo's quarters. The path led between the two, to a drive, also deserted, and a garage, its doors wide open.

Perhaps he had driven into Mahon. Lucy retraced her steps. She crossed the main courtyard. The tap of her sandals sounded unnervingly loud on the flagstones. She reached the sliding glass doors to the living-room. They were closed, but not locked, the frame slid back smoothly to her touch.

Surely someone was there. Laurent was so edgy about his privacy, not to say paranoid about security: he surely wouldn't go out, leaving his home unlocked and unguarded. Lucy called out again. She crossed the room and shouted down the steps to the corridor beyond. Her voice seemed to echo in the silence.

Then she heard a strange clicking noise, somewhere behind her. She whirled round.

'Freeze!' The shout reached her in mid-turn. She had to finish the movement, but the instruction sank in quickly, and she froze as soon as she had turned.

It was Alonzo. He was standing, feet apart, in the middle of the elegant white room. There was a gun in his hand, and it was pointing right at her.

'Hands up!' he said, in his thick Catalan accent.

Lucy's hands moved unsteadily above her head. Heavens! She had thought this only happened in films.

Alonzo gestured with the gun. She edged awkwardly away from the corridor, and into the room. 'Sit!' he snapped at her. She sat on one of the low leather sofas. She was shaking.

'Stay there.'

Alonzo backed towards a doorway, and appeared to press some kind of a button. There was the shrill buzz of an alarm bell, sounding elsewhere in the house. It echoed around Lucy's head. She couldn't believe that this was really happening to her.

Alonzo returned to his position in front of her, and angled his gun once more. Behind her, Lucy could hear someone coming down the corridor, their footsteps loud on the tiled floor.

'What's going on?' It was Laurent's voice. Something seemed to snap inside Lucy. Unthinkingly, she jumped to her feet, and dashed to the safety of his arms.

They wrapped round her, firm and reassuring. Everything else seemed like a nightmare, but this was real, surely. Laurent was real.

She could feel his heart thudding through his shirt, from where she was caught against his chest. The steady rhythm of it drowned out everything else. Somewhere, someone was talking. Loudly, angrily. It came back into her head only slowly that this was Alonzo, and that Alonzo still had a gun.

Her body froze once more. She was safe here, surely, in Laurent's arms, but if she was to move again...

Laurent was talking now, his voice quiet and firm, its tone commanding. He was speaking in Castilian; Lucy didn't even try to follow him. Alonzo replied, Laurent spoke again. Then there were footsteps, and a long silence.

'Lucy,' Laurent said gently.

Slowly, painfully slowly, she brought her head up to look at him.

Those liquid brown eyes looked straight down into hers. 'It's all right, Lucy,' Laurent said. 'He's gone now.'

The impulse that had held her frozen deserted her with alarming suddenness. She could feel her body crumpling, but she didn't seem to be able to do anything to stop it. Fortunately Laurent acted for her, picking her up in two strong arms, and carrying her back over to the sofa.

The world was whirling. Lucy closed her eyes, to shut it out.

The next thing she knew was Laurent's voice, saying firmly, 'Here. Drink this.' She half opened her eyes, and he set down the glass he was holding and pulled her up to a sitting position. Then he held her firmly by the shoulders as he supervised her downing of a sizeable glass of brandy.

Brandy, Lucy thought weakly. Oh, dear. Every time she came to Laurent's villa she seemed to end up collapsing and being revived by his brandy.

Slowly, the cogs of her mind slid back into gear. Alonzo. A gun. Laurent, commanding. The pattern these pieces made was not a reassuring one.

It struck her, suddenly, that what had seemed like a safe harbour was in reality rather more like a keg of gunpowder.

She tried to struggle to her feet, but Laurent's arm was like a vice around her shoulders, and she barely managed to lift herself from the sofa.

'Not yet,' he said firmly.

Not yet? But she couldn't stay here, in the arms of a man whose servant had just pointed a gun at her! Heavens, if she had wanted confirmation that Laurent was up to no good, she had certainly been given it.

She took a deep breath. 'Please let me go,' she said, in a very unsteady voice.

'You're in no state to go anywhere. You're quite safe with me. Alonzo has gone. He never meant to frighten you so. It was all a misunderstanding.'

A misunderstanding! There seemed to be an awful lot of misunderstandings where she and Laurent were concerned, Lucy thought to herself, and all of them struck her as acutely dangerous.

'Let me go,' she repeated.

'I'll let go of you now, if you promise not to move. Then in a moment, when you are recovered, I will take you back home. I can explain everything, I promise you.'

Explain! There were no explanations, in Lucy's world, that covered threats and men with guns. If Laurent lived in a world like this, she wanted to be out of it as quickly as possible. Every instinct told her that she was in terrible danger as long as she remained at the villa. She had to get out of it, to get right away from him. But she wouldn't escape by brute force, she would have to use cunning.

'I promise,' she whispered.

Slowly, the pressure of his arm across her shoulders eased. He brought his other hand over, and took hold of hers.

'God, you're cold,' he said matter-of-factly. 'I think you must be in shock. You really ought to lie down for a while. You can use my bedroom. I'll lock the doors, so you can be quite sure you will be safe.'

Use his bedroom? Lucy numbly shook her head. She didn't dare to meet Laurent's eyes again. Cautiously, she glanced towards the glass doors. She had left them open when she walked through. Laurent and Alonzo had come along the corridor. They hadn't closed the doors: there was an open space between the two sections of aluminium framing.

How far? Round the other sofa and to the doors was perhaps a dozen paces. Then she had to get through the doors and across the courtyard, down the steps, along the quay. Untying the *Sophie* would be the hard part. She would need a good head start, or she wouldn't have any real hope of doing that before either Laurent or Alonzo caught up with her. She didn't think there was anyone else in the house—except possibly Juana, but she was too plump to move fast.

Her eyes moved to the brown legs exposed by Laurent's shorts. She could see the hard muscles of his thighs and calves. He was a good ten years older than she, but he was a man, and very fit.

A plan of sorts came to her. It was a long shot, but the best she could think of. She said, in a voice whose weakness she didn't need to feign, 'I think I need a little more brandy.'

'Just a little, perhaps,' Laurent said. He picked up the glass. He squeezed her hand, then stood up. She heard him move over to the cupboards where the decanter was.

She had to turn and watch him, to be sure of getting the moment right. Now—he had his back to her and was pouring brandy. She had a four or five paces' lead, no more. Half crouching, she began to move towards the door.

He saw her just before she reached it.

'Lucy!'

Lucy heard the sound of splintering glass, but no more, because she was running now, running faster than she had ever run before. The blood seemed to pound in her head. She sprinted across the courtyard, past the swimming pool. Along the path that led to the clifftop. There were the steps. Down, down.

'Lucy!'

The shout was close behind her. She had to go faster, faster. She took the steps three and four at a time. A turn, by the lower terrace, and another flight.

Her foot caught, on the loose edge of the board that formed the top step. There was a moment of sheer terror as she hurtled forwards. Then came nothing but blackness.

CHAPTER SIX

WHEN Lucy woke, she was in a bed, a very comfortable bed, with a firm mattress and a soft bolster and crisp, cool sheets surrounding her.

She took in these sensations, then slowly opened her eyes. A strange room. A bedroom, of course. Three white walls, and one wall of glass, through which sunlight streamed.

Laurent's villa. It all came back to her, and she sat up abruptly. That was a mistake. It felt as if she had slammed her head into a brick wall. The pain hit her, thick and ugly, and she fell back on to the pillows. At the same time, somebody who had been sitting by the bed stood up.

The thumping pain subsided. Slowly, so as not to bring it back, Lucy turned her head.

She met the enquiring button eyes of Juana, who said, in very slow Castilian, 'So, you are awake. I call Señor Buckley.'

So, I am awake, Lucy thought, turning her head again. Who on earth was Señor Buckley? It seemed a very difficult question. She closed her eyes again, and the question drifted away with her consciousness.

She dreamed, this time. Laurent was there, and he was holding her to him. She looked up, up to his face—he was incredibly tall, in the dream—and he bent to kiss her. Then his face, as it came closer to hers, seemed to change in shape. It slowly metamorphosed from a handsome man into a sneering wolf. The wolf-face moved closer and closer and closer...

'Gently,' said a commanding voice, cutting through something that sounded like a scream. 'You're fine now. Gently, gently, Lucy.'

Lucy's mouth shut, and the scream stopped. Had it been her scream? She hadn't been aware of screaming. She felt firm hands on her arms. She had been sitting up. The firm hands gently pressed her down on to the pillows.

Laurent's hands. Laurent's face. No wolf now, just Laurent, looking grim and worried.

'Perhaps you should have a sedative,' said Laurent. 'I told the doctor not to give you anything until you came round. Don't move, I'll just go to call him.'

'The doctor...'

'He's in the next room. I'll be right back.'

Lucy waited limply for him to come back. With him was the doctor, a short, dapper young man. She lay back and listened to the doctor and Laurent talking in a language that she knew was Spanish, but somehow could not understand. Then the doctor approached the bed. He said in slow, heavily accented English, 'There is nothing to fear. This will make you sleep.'

It did.

She woke again, to darkness. And again, to find Sophie sitting by the bed.

'Morning,' Sophie said cheerfully.

'Morning,' Lucy echoed. Morning, she thought. Was it really? The sunlight was there to confirm it.

'How are you feeling?'

It was difficult to tell, lying flat. Very slowly, Lucy sat up.

'Better, I think,' she said.

'That's good. The doctor said it was only mild concussion, and a few cuts and bruises. The railing came off worst out of the encounter.'

'Railing?'

'Along the steps down to the harbour. You probably don't remember. You came to Laurent's villa yesterday to explain why you'd missed him the night before, and you lost your footing on the steps and fell.'

'And fell.'

Sophie grinned. 'You idiot! If I'd had any idea you were going to take the *Sophie* I'd have tied you to the bedpost. Still, you certainly managed to grab his attention.'

Lucy lay back on the pillows. It was coming back to her, yet again. Had she really fallen? She couldn't remember that bit. But she could remember sailing over to the villa; she could remember Alonzo and the gun.

The gun. Laurent couldn't have told Sophie anything about the gun. So Sophie was sitting here in his villa, calm as a melon, knowing nothing about the gun, and nothing about the danger they both were in.

'Sophie,' she said weakly, 'we have to go.'

'Do we?' Sophie asked. 'Well, I do, pretty soon. I need to get back to the kids before they drive Señora Ribero bananas. But I'm sure Laurent won't let you go till you're properly recovered. It's all very respectable, there's nothing to worry about. There's a woman called Juana here, she'll look after you. Really

I needn't have come at all, I suppose, but Laurent thought you'd like me to be here when you woke up.'

'I'd rather go now, with you.'

Sophie shook her head. 'I shouldn't think Laurent would let you. He's very masterful, isn't he? Not my type at all, but I can see why you went for him. He's been really worried about you, Lucy. He won't let you go anywhere till the doctor gives the all clear.'

Lucy stared helplessly at her. She knew it was important to make Sophie understand, but it all seemed much, much too difficult.

Sophie stood up. 'I'll call him now,' she said, 'and he can tell you himself. He's been waiting for me to tell him you're awake.'

'Oh, no,' Lucy murmured.

Sophie stopped half-way to the glass doors, and glanced at her. 'I shouldn't worry,' she said cheerfully. 'You don't look nearly as bad as you probably think. A bit unkempt, perhaps, but that pale and interesting look suits you. It'll bring out all his strong protective instincts, you wait and see.'

Lucy still hadn't thought of an answer to this when Sophie disappeared through the door.

She reappeared a few moments later, with Laurent. Lucy looked helplessly at him. It was just Laurent, a man she had met in a bar. He was wearing a white shirt and trousers, and he didn't look like a gun-slinger or a wolf or a monster, just like a handsome man on holiday in the sun. He came quickly over to the bed, and took her hands before she could pull them away.

'Feeling better?' he asked.

Lucy tried to tell herself that behind that worried look and that reassuring voice there was a dangerous man, but it just didn't make sense. She closed her eyes, to shut him out.

'I want to go home,' she said.

'Of course you do. The doctor should be here in twenty minutes. If he gives his OK then, Sophie will drive you home, and you can get back to bed when you arrive in Villa Carlos. If that's all right with you, Sophie?'

'Sounds reasonable,' Sophie said.

'Juana is very willing to look after you here, but I can see that you would prefer to be at home.'

He could see that? She wasn't trapped, wasn't a prisoner here in his villa? There had to be catch hidden in his words. Lucy tried to think where it was, but she couldn't see how there could be one, when Sophie hadn't noticed it.

'I'll leave you with Sophie now, but I'll see you again before you go.'

Lucy opened her eyes, met his unnerving gaze, and shut them again.

'Yes,' she murmured.

'And I'll send Juana along with some coffee and rolls for breakfast. The doctor said you ought to eat when you woke.'

'No,' murmured Lucy.

'Yes,' Sophie briskly corrected her.

An hour and a half later, Lucy was lying in her bed at Sophie and Juan's villa. Laurent had let her leave without a murmur, though he had extracted a promise from Sophie that she would phone him from the call box that evening to tell him how Lucy was feeling. Sophie, driving erratically through Mahon on the way home, had been loud in her praise of the way he had handled the little accident.

Lucy had thought of telling her about the gun. She had a strong suspicion that Sophie wouldn't believe her. She hardly believed it herself by now. Perhaps it had been part of the nightmare. Anyway, the nightmare was over now. The rest of that day in bed, one more day taking things gently, and then, the doctor had said, she would be able to get back to work.

Lucy stood at the stern of the *San Felipe*, helping passengers off the gangplank and into the boat, and checking their tickets. It was three-twenty, ten minutes before the harbour tour was due to leave, and there was a little queue of holiday-makers snaking back over the concrete of the quayside.

A blond couple, in matching shorts. German? '*Deutsch?*' Lucy ventured, and was rewarded with two smiles. An English family she recognised; they were staying at the Don Carlos. She warned the mother to keep an eye on her little girl because of the deep water out in the harbour, and turned to the next passenger.

Oh, no. It couldn't be Laurent.

It was.

'But you can't...I'm working,' Lucy said helplessly.

'I do have a ticket.' Laurent held out his hand.

Numbly, Lucy looked. He did have a ticket. She hadn't sold it to him; Juan must have done, or Sophie, or Vanessa. Whichever of them it had been, she would happily have killed them all right then.

Laurent jumped into the boat. He looked past Lucy and nodded at Juan, and then settled himself on the bench that ran along the far side.

Lucy stared at him. 'Miss,' a sharp female voice said from behind her. She turned guiltily to see to the next passengers.

Somehow she got them all boarded. Somehow she managed to go through the motions of casting off. Somehow she picked up her microphone. She looked at Laurent then—that was a mistake. His eyes were fixed on her, and she stumbled over her greetings. Laurent carefully moved his glance and stared intently up at the clifftops.

Lucy pulled herself together, and tightened her grip on the microphone.

'Welcome to our tour of Mahon harbour, ladies and gentlemen. If you look to your right, you will see a big red house standing at the very corner of the promontory. You see it now? Now look left, and you'll see its twin on the opposite side of this bay. Those are the customs houses, relics of the English occupation of Minorca. The English governed this island for a century, with a few short breaks, from 1708 until 1802. They were responsible for moving the capital of the island from Ciudadela on the west coast to Mahon on the east. They also built most of Villa Carlos. Take a look when we get back to the town, and you'll see that many of the houses have sash windows, just like in an English Georgian seaside resort. They are unique in Spain; you'll see them in no other town. The barracks in the square in the town centre were built for English soldiers, though Spanish soldiers now guard them. In those days, of course, Villa Carlos had a different name. The English called it Georgetown, after their then King, George III.'

She knew the words by heart; it was reassuring repeating them. *Deutsch*. Yes, do it in German. She hadn't noticed any French passengers, but she said it all in French too, to keep herself busy.

By then they were chugging along the main harbourside, towards the fish restaurant where she and Laurent had dined together a lifetime before. Lucy set down her microphone for a moment.

How could he? she thought. How dared he? Worse, why hadn't she guessed he would, and steeled herself to be ready for it? She might have known, when she had refused to speak to him on the phone ever since she had left his villa, that he would find some other way of contacting her. It was, she admitted reluctantly, the ideal way. On the *San Felipe* she couldn't possibly avoid him.

But he couldn't possibly talk seriously to her either. He couldn't spin her any explanations about the gun, not with thirty-odd tourists listening. Ironically, she was probably safer from him on the *San Felipe* than she would have been anywhere else.

She told herself this, as firmly as she could, and went on to the next part of her commentary.

'This great harbour has seen three thousand years of history, ladies and gentlemen. The Phoenicians founded Mahon, perhaps around 1200 BC, though there are now no significant remains of their occupation to be seen. Then the Greeks invaded, followed in turn by the Carthaginians, the Romans, the Vandals, the Byzantines, the Arabs, the Normans and the Spanish. This harbour has been fought over as intensively as any in the world. All the Mediterranean island harbours are useful, but perhaps those early invaders did not realise how very special this one is. It is one of the finest deep-water harbours in the world, second largest only to Pearl Harbor in the Pacific. You will see, as we go further up the harbour, how even the largest ships can sail right up it, and unload their cargoes directly on to a main road.'

She felt confident enough after this spiel to glance at Laurent. He still appeared to be absorbed in the view. She went on to the German version.

Juan swung the boat round the blunt tip of the harbour, and began the slow trawl down the north-eastern shore. He steered a few yards further out from the shore as they approached Laurent's villa.

The *Santa Caterina* was moored at the wooden jetty. Lucy glanced at the hillside beyond it. The railings along the steps up to the villa had already been repaired.

The *San Felipe* moved on. It slid down the narrow canal, no wider than a typical English river, that sep-arated the Lazareto from the mainland to its north-east. It rounded the island and ventured into the open Mediterranean. It swung back towards the harbour mouth. Lucy began to hand round the plastic glasses and the bottles of sticky liqueurs.

Juan turned into the Cala St Esteban, the big bay just off the mouth to the harbour, and cut the engine. At the end of the bay a few holiday-makers were swimming in the clear water. Lucy tried to concen-trate on them, but her eyes kept wandering back to Laurent. He was talking politely to the English couple with the small daughter, and holding a little cup of gin and lemonade which he had barely sipped.

The last stage of the trip went quickly, too quickly for Lucy's liking. Laurent couldn't talk to her on the boat, that was obvious, but it was equally obvious that he had come on the harbour tour with every intention of finding some opportunity to talk to her. She didn't expect to get off lightly once the *San Felipe* reached its moorings.

The little pleasure-boat chugged up its home bay. Lucy jumped off it as usual, helped Juan to moor it close to the quayside, set up the gangplank and helped the other passengers off. Laurent didn't follow them. Lucy turned to look at him. He got up from the bench and went to talk to Juan. They had a short conversation, their voices too low for her to catch any of the words. Juan finished it with a nod and a smile, and moved towards Lucy at the stern of the boat.

'I'll be back in ten minutes,' he said. He disembarked, and disappeared in the direction of his hut.

Lucy gazed despairingly after him. It was her job to clear up the debris and lock away the drinks; she couldn't leave the boat yet, and she couldn't escape from Laurent either. He was already vaulting off the stern and striding across the short stretch of concrete that separated them.

'Now perhaps you'll listen to me.'

'Go away. Please.'

'Not till I've explained to you.'

'There isn't any need for that.' Lucy set her chin firmly, and turned her face away from him.

'I think there is.' He took her by the wrist, and pulled lightly on it, drawing her closer to the boat.

'Heaven knows what you think I'm up to. I can see your imagination is working overtime.'

Lucy didn't reply. Come back quickly, Juan, her mind urged. She wished now that she had told Juan and Sophie about the gun. Surely if he had known what had really happened at Laurent's villa, Juan wouldn't have left her in this ghastly predicament.

'Alonzo is back at my villa,' Laurent said calmly, 'and you can see that I am not armed. Frisk me if you like.'

Lucy shook her head.

'Then come and sit down. There's nothing to be frightened of. Juan will be watching us all the time, and if you don't believe my explanation you need never see me again.'

Believe him? She wasn't going to see him again whether she believed him or not; nothing, nothing was more certain than that. Except the fact that Laurent wasn't going to leave her until he'd said his piece. So she might as well get it over with, Lucy told herself, and be done with him.

'All right,' she said grudgingly, pulling her hand free. She got back on to the boat. Laurent followed her on board. They both sat down on the slatted wooden bench at the stern, in the shade of the striped awning. Laurent reached for her hand again, but she quickly moved it away, and he didn't persist.

'You must think both my and Alonzo's behaviour quite unforgivable,' he said in a steady voice. 'I have no doubt that in your place I should think the same. But there is a rational explanation for everything that happened, and even if you find yourself unable to forgive me, I think it would reassure you if you knew it.'

Lucy didn't answer, and he went on, 'As your friend Anna told you, I'm a banker. I head a division of Brown and Lefèvre, a merchant bank in Paris—the division that deals with new share issues. Over the last year or so we have been handling some politically controversial issues for the French government. The government are part-privatising various nationalised companies. It's a policy that left-wing politicians strongly disapprove of, and as a result of our involvement the bank has attracted some abrasive publicity.'

'I've heard about that,' Lucy said nervously. 'An aerospace company, wasn't it, and...'

She sensed Laurent's little start of surprise. 'That's right,' he said. '*Aerospatiale de France*, and part of the SNCF. I was in charge of both of those deals.'

'But what has that to do with...?'

'I'm coming to that. There's been a lot of publicity about the share deals in the financial Press all over Europe, but particularly in France, and as a result my name became known to a left-wing terrorist organisation, one whose members violently oppose the government policy. They made some telephone threats to the bank, to try to scare us into pulling out of the deals. Then when those didn't work they sent a written threat to have me killed if we persisted in handling the work.'

'Killed?'

She didn't pull away her hand this time when he reached for it. Her eyes lifted instinctively to his face. His met them readily. He isn't lying, she thought with sudden, total conviction; he isn't spinning me a tale. All this is absolutely true.

'It sounds horrendous, I know,' he said. 'Enough to give anyone nightmares. But in reality it's not so very alarming. The police assured me that literally thousands of people in public life receive similar letters every year.'

'But to kill you, just because of a share deal . . .'

'It's incomprehensible, I know, to most normal people. But to these fanatics the privatisation policy is a vital symptom of the capitalist conspiracy against the honest working people of France.' He gave an edgy laugh. 'The threats were undoubtedly a genuine attempt to make the bank change its mind about accepting the business. That didn't mean that the terrorists would necessarily have carried them out, though; most such threats are pretty empty.'

'So you weren't really in danger . . .' Lucy said slowly. At the same time, her brain was working feverishly. Kill Laurent, it kept repeating. Kill Laurent! Oh, no, no, no, no . . .

'Probably not,' Laurent agreed. He squeezed her hand reassuringly. 'I'm still alive, as you see! But though most death threats are no more than bluffs, there are occasional exceptions. Naturally I took the letter immediately to the police, and they advised me that this particular terrorist group has actually carried out a few politically motivated assassinations over the past few years.'

Lucy went cold. Kill Laurent, she thought. Kill Laurent. He had known it himself, that sensation of having a gun pointed straight at him. Only in his case it hadn't been a single moment of terror, it had been a nameless, invisible threat hanging over him all the time. Any moment, he must have thought, any moment the bullet might hit me. Must *have* thought? Heavens, he must still be thinking it!

'Lucy,' Laurent said gently, 'it's all over now. I promise you, it's over. No more danger, for me or for you.'

The even, reassuring voice stabbed through the layers of terror reverberating round her brain. Over. 'My God,' she murmured.

'Look—oh, come here!' he exclaimed, suddenly impatient. He reached out for her, pulling her hard against him. Lucy stretched out her arms and squeezed them tight around him. She could feel him, solid and warm and very definitely alive against her. They sat like that, holding each other as tightly as they could, for what seemed like a long time.

Slowly, slowly, Laurent's grip eased. 'Better now?' he asked in a low voice.

'I think so,' Lucy said unsteadily. She brought a hand to the back of her head.

'Head aching?'

'I don't think so.'

He laughed at her reply. Somehow it broke the tension, and Lucy found herself laughing too, and reaching for him again.

'It's not that,' she said, when she had recovered enough to speak again, 'it's just that it seems so...'

'So unreal,' Laurent finished for her. 'I know. That's how it seemed to me, when I first opened the letter in my office and read those preposterous threats. Sometimes it just seems all too stupid for words, and then sometimes you find yourself thinking, good lord, they mean it, and your blood runs cold.'

'That's how it was,' Lucy agreed. 'But it really is over now?'

'It really is,' Laurent said firmly. 'Look, poor Juan is still waiting for us. I'd better just let him know it's OK now, and then he can get going. Then I'll tell you the rest of the story, and afterwards I'll drive you home myself.'

Lucy looked over his shoulder. There was Juan, lounging outside his hut—closed now—and very obviously waiting for the two of them.

'It *is* OK?' Laurent added, more uncertainly.

'It is.'

She watched Laurent jump down from the stern of the *San Felipe*, and walk over to Juan. She saw Juan grin, and slap him cheerfully on the shoulder. Then Juan moved off towards his car, and Laurent made his way back towards her in the boat.

She seemed to see every detail of his appearance with heightened intensity, as if the threat of his death, evaded, made him twice as alive to her. And twice as wonderful, because she was beginning to be sure now that he wasn't the monster of her nightmare, and that the rest of his story would explain everything to her.

Everything about him pleased her: his easy, loose-limbed walk, the casually elegant striped shirt and white trousers, the brown of his skin, so dark against them, the sinews of his arm, standing out clearly as he set his hand on the stern of the boat and vaulted in to join her.

He took in the intentness of her look, and smiled at her. They sat for a moment, just looking at each other. Then, very gently, Laurent reached forward and caught hold of a hank of her hair. He drew her face towards his, and lightly, lightly, let his lips rest on hers.

Lucy didn't try to intensify the contact. It was enough just to know that he was here, he was alive. And surely, surely, he was hers.

'You do want to hear the rest?' he asked.

'Please.'

'OK. Well, as I said, there was always just an outside chance that the threat wasn't a bluff, so the police advised me to be very careful until the whole thing blew over. They suggested I leave Paris for a while, and asked me if there was anywhere else I might go. I told them about the villa. Catherine bought it— that's my ex-wife—last year, but I'd never even been here before. And straight away they told me it would be the ideal place for me to come. Minorca's such a small, quiet island, it would be extremely difficult for known terrorists to land here without being spotted.'

'So you came.'

He nodded. 'As soon as I could; as soon as all the urgent work connected with the deals was over. I wasn't going to let the terrorists frighten me out of finishing that, but I could see the sense in being cautious once it was done.

'For the first ten days I never budged outside the villa. By then I was bored stiff. I'm not used to lounging around; I hadn't taken a holiday for years, and I've never been the sort of person who can laze by a pool for hours on end. So I asked the local police if it would be safe to venture out, and they told me they reckoned it would. Obviously I didn't want to make myself conspicuous, so I chose to go for a drink in a quiet bar in a quiet bay.'

'Mal's.'

'That's right.'

'And straight away you walked into a conversation about your villa and your power-boat!'

Laurent gave a rueful grin. 'I thought for a moment that I really had become paranoid. A white speed-boat: I told myself it couldn't have been the *Santa Caterina*. But I checked with Alonzo the next morning, and realised that it had been.'

'Why?' Lucy frowned. 'Why did he do it?'

Laurent shrugged. 'A misjudgement, I guess you'd call it. I hired Alonzo as a kind of watchdog, as well as a handyman for the villa. The police put me on to him. I've a suspicion he has a criminal record himself, but that didn't worry me unduly: it made it all the more likely that he would pick up anything suspicious going on. We went over the security arrangements at the villa, and I mentioned to him that I was unhappy about the boats in the harbour. Catherine had told me the villa was on the waterfront, but it hadn't dawned on me that there would be a solid procession of boats past the foot of my garden all day long. I wondered out loud whether there was anything that could be done to keep them a little further from the shoreline, and . . .'

'And that's what Alonzo did.'

'That's one of the things he did. He managed to shoo the yachts away quite easily, and then he started on the pleasure-boats.'

It made sense. It all made sense now. Blundering Alonzo, doing his best to ensure Laurent's safety;

Laurent's concern when he discovered that Alonzo's efforts had only served to trigger Lucy's curiosity; his even greater concern when she had told him of Anna's commentaries. It would have been the last thing he wanted, she could see now, to have the boat guides pointing out his address to boatloads of strangers every day.

'But it all misfired,' Lucy said slowly.

'It certainly seemed to be doing. After you told me about Anna I hesitated to venture out again, even to take you to dinner. And then, when Alonzo caught you at the villa...'

'He imagined the worst,' Lucy said.

'I don't think he even stopped to imagine, he just reacted. Actually you were in no danger—the gun wasn't loaded. I know it must have been terrifying for you, but I can't blame Alonzo for it. He has been doing his best to carry out my instructions. And I hope you'll understand that though I've spoken very sternly to him, I can't possibly fire him in the circumstances.'

'Of course not,' Lucy agreed. She didn't like the idea of encountering Alonzo again, but she could see the sense in what Laurent said. She thought some more. 'What I still don't understand,' she said slowly, 'is why you're safe now.'

'That's all happened over the last twenty-four hours. It shook me so, when you ran from the villa and had that terrible fall. It's so lucky that it was only concussion, but I couldn't help thinking that it might have been much, much worse. And afterwards, waiting for you to recover, I thought, I can't go on

like this. I can't keep up a fence against the rest of
the world for ever. I had to reconsider the situation.

'So I talked to the police in Mahon, and to the Paris
police, and to my contacts in Interpol, and managed
to stir them up enough to get them to check out the
situation thoroughly.'

'And they told you that you were safe.'

'That's what it comes to, yes.' Laurent gave an
awkward grin. 'It's a combination of things, really. I
think by then I *had* become more than a little
paranoid. Rationally, for instance, I should have seen
that Anna and the other boat guides wouldn't think
me particularly interesting to their passengers, and
that they were hardly likely to trouble to mention me
by name. Instead of telling myself that the police were
erring on the side of caution, I'd done everything they
advised to protect myself, and twice as much again.

'For another thing, the threat really had receded.
If the terrorists had planned to kill me, they would
have acted fairly swiftly, as soon as it was apparent
that I wouldn't respond to the letter. The share deals
are old news by now. Then finally the Paris police
told me that they've had all the suspected terrorists
under close observation for the past few weeks, and
they've concluded now that the threat was definitely
an empty one.'

'Definitely?'

'Definitely. The suspects have done nothing that
might suggest otherwise, nothing at all. They haven't
even surveyed the bank, let alone pursued me to
Minorca. And they've now turned their attention to
a different issue, and have been writing similar letters
to officials in the Ministry of the Interior.'

'Poor officials,' Lucy said feelingly.

'Absolutely. But lucky me.'

'And me!'

Laurent laughed. He kissed her again, the pressure of his lips harder this time. 'Come on,' he said. 'Juan and Sophie must be wondering where you've got to. I'll take you back to the villa, and then if you feel up to it, perhaps we can go on to have supper together.'

'Laurent,' Lucy assured him, 'I feel wonderful.'

CHAPTER SEVEN

'I WON'T be long,' Lucy assured Laurent, as she left him at the foot of the stairs in the villa.

'No need to hurry. Sophie will take care of me.'

I bet she will, Lucy thought, watching him disappear towards the kitchen, clearly perfectly at home in Sophie and Juan's house. What woman wouldn't?

And how much he needed caring for! Her heart ached at the thought of all he must have gone through that summer. As far as she knew, he didn't have anyone like Sophie and Juan to whom he had been able to turn for reassurance; there had only been Alonzo between him and disaster. How terribly alone he must have felt when he had read that appalling letter. How isolated he must have been, coming to a strange island, to a house his ex-wife had bought, a house to which she had come without him the year before. Stupid, stupid woman. Imagine any woman leaving Laurent!

She, Lucy, wouldn't, that was for certain. But she wouldn't win him in the first place, if she stood there mooning all night! She hastily abandoned her reverie, and hurried upstairs to get ready for their date.

Laurent wouldn't have any opportunity to change, so she would have to wear something that matched his casual shirt and trousers. She flicked through her smallish holiday wardrobe, and finally settled on a bright blue dress that buttoned down the front. Its

low V-neck meant she couldn't wear a bra under it;
she eyed her outline critically, thankful that her
breasts, smallish and firm, didn't really need the
support.

Was there time to put up her hair? No, he didn't
like her with her hair up, he liked her Cinderella look.
She spent five minutes brushing out the tangles it had
acquired on the boat, thankful that she had washed
it early that morning. He liked her to look natural,
but that didn't mean that nature couldn't be given a
subtle helping hand, so she carefully outlined her green
eyes with a touch of blue liner, and spread some con-
cealer over the fading bruise on her temple. That was
right—simple, relaxed. He would be more relaxed
himself now, surely. He wouldn't have that tense,
anxious look about him now he knew he was safe.

He wouldn't have to keep her at her distance any
more. Their holiday romance could begin in earnest.
And at the same time she could start in earnest to see
if there would be any opportunity to turn it into
something longer lasting.

He didn't mean to marry again, he had said. A depressing thought, but all divorced men said that at
first, surely? Perhaps the events of the summer would
convince him that he needed a permanent woman in
his life, someone to confide in, someone to relax with.

A banker. Not just any banker, a *merchant* banker.
A division head at Brown and Lefèvre. Lucy had heard
of Brown and Lefèvre, a large and highly reputed international banking house. They were just the kind
of company she wanted to work for herself after she
graduated.

What would Laurent think, she wondered, when she told him that it was her own ambition to go into merchant banking? Tense and secretive as he had been, he hadn't encouraged her to tell him any more about herself than he had told her about himself. Now she would have a chance to burrow beneath the superficial holiday chat, and to find out about his real thoughts and feelings, his ideas, his hopes and fears. Now she would have a chance to tell him about the real Lucy. Of course, the Lucy he already knew was a real Lucy in a sense, but there was another Lucy, the Lucy who lived in grey northern cities, who was just as real, and who was there for a great deal more of the time.

She slicked on just a touch of pink lipstick, rubbed half of it away again, and dashed downstairs.

Laurent was in the front room, talking to Sophie, apparently unperturbed by the blaring television, by the heated argument Manuel and Maria were pursuing, and by Cara's squeals as Juan bounced her on his knee.

He turned and looked her up and down. Lucy posed, a little self-consciously, for his inspection. There was something sophisticated about the appraising way he looked at her. He was so different from Hugh, and from the boys she knew at university. It was surprising, she thought, that he should like her best when she looked her most casual. She would have thought he would go for a sleek career-girl look: expensive but understated little suits, linen dresses, one good piece of jewellery. Hair up, not down. Perhaps he would prefer her to dress like that in Paris.

But they weren't in Paris, they were on Minorca, and the sun was still shining, the sky was blue. 'Where are we going?' she asked brightly.

'Ciudadela. Or so Sophie advises me.'

'Fine.'

Juan turned to her, and grunted, 'And be back by...'

'Midnight? Oh, Juan, can't I make it one o'clock, just for tonight?'

'Lucy, love,' Sophie said, 'it's only a day since you were an invalid in bed. Twelve, OK?'

Must they treat her like a schoolgirl in front of Laurent? Lucy thought rebelliously. But Sophie did have a point: the buzz in her head that wasn't quite a headache wasn't going to stay under control for ever.

'OK,' Laurent said firmly. 'Bye, kids.'

'Bye,' the kids chorused, as he and Lucy made their way to the door.

'Does Manuel remind you of Gilles?' Lucy asked, once they were in Laurent's car.

'Gilles?' He glanced at her with a little frown, as if he had forgotten that he had mentioned his son to her. 'Not particularly.'

That wasn't exactly outgoing and relaxed, that was a brush-off. Perhaps she was being too nosey, too quickly. She hurriedly turned the conversation.

'Of course I never had a chance to apologise properly for standing you up on our last date.'

'Oh, Sophie explained that she hadn't passed on the note. I knew it wasn't a very reliable way of getting in contact with you. I meant to phone, but I couldn't track down the number.'

'Sophie and Juan aren't on the phone. Sophie hates telephones, and Juan doesn't seem to mind doing without.' Lucy went on to explain about her long day out.

'I'm glad it wasn't anything serious,' Laurent said. 'Sophie didn't seem at all worried, but from what she said it wasn't like you to be so late without giving her warning.'

'No, it isn't.' Lucy giggled, a little nervously. 'You must think I'm a walking disaster zone: falling into the harbour, hurtling down the villa steps, getting stranded in the middle of the island with no petrol. But really I'm a very cool, calm, collected person.'

'Really?' Laurent said, in a teasing voice.

Lucy privately cursed. It would hardly be surprising, she thought, if he *did* think that. It obviously wasn't the moment to try and present him with an image of herself as a promising career woman—he would probably hoot with laughter.

'Have you been to Ciudadela before?' she asked instead.

'Never. Tell me about it.'

Lucy started to tell him about the old capital of the island. They would be there in under an hour, and she thought she might take the opportunity to show him some of the old buildings before the sun went down. Ciudadela was an older town than Mahon, she explained, and it still had many medieval buildings in the Moorish style. She described some of the tourist sights that would be closed to visitors when they arrived: the cathedral, the town hall with its lovely terrace overlooking the harbour, and the Bishop's Palace.

While she talked, Laurent drove: fast but carefully, along the winding road that led across the full width of the island from Mahon in the east to Ciudadela in the west. He hadn't been to the old capital before, but the road was easy to follow, passing through just three small towns, like Alayor, that were really little more than villages.

They parked in a side street not far from the town centre of Ciudadela, and Lucy led the way through the narrow streets, lined with tall buildings ornately carved from soft yellowish stone. She showed Laurent the arcades around the cathedral which now housed modern boutiques, crowded in the early evening; the tree-lined Plaza d'es Born, surrounded by the great civic buildings and the palaces of the old nobility; the view down to the long narrow harbour, with its yachts and harbourside restaurants. They even peeped round some of the open doors of the old houses that had been converted to offices, and glimpsed vast cool stone halls, with huge stairways spiralling up to plant-lined landings.

'Wonderful stuff,' Laurent said. 'Such a pleasure after the concrete blocks of Mahon. It makes me sorry, really, that my own villa isn't in this area. It was Catherine's choice for the villa, that bland international style; it's functional, but I don't find it particularly attractive.'

'I'm glad,' Lucy said, 'because I completely agree with you there. It was a dream of mine, the first time I saw these houses, to live in one just like them. But I don't think many of them are used as holiday homes—the international agents don't seem to handle them. And they probably demand more upkeep than is practicable for an occasional home.'

'Maybe so,' Laurent agreed. 'Are you ready to eat now?'

'There's just one more place I want to show you.'

Vanessa had once taken Lucy to a bar, out at the far edge of the old town, in a building that had been an old mill. The mill itself, sailless but unmistakable, still towered above, and its circular base dominated the bar below. In the stone vaults around the base, Minorcan men played at cards, with cigarettes drooping from their mouths and little glasses of brandy waiting next to the piles of pesetas at their elbows.

'You always avoid the tourist haunts, don't you?' Laurent asked, when they had found a corner to sit with their tiny cups of muddy coffee.

Lucy said, 'There are tourists everywhere on Minorca. It's one of the pleasures of the island, that they are never made to feel unwelcome. But I do like the bars like this, where the locals outnumber them. The locals know the best places, anyway; the tourists often don't find them.'

She watched as Laurent took another look around the bar. Though it was picturesque, it was scruffy even by the moderate standards of Ciudadela; but she had assumed that he would feel as comfortable here as he would in a flash Paris restaurant. She could tell by his expression that she had been right.

'I haven't seen a flamenco dancer since I came to the island,' he mused.

'A few perform in the big hotels. They're quite fun to watch, though it's done unashamedly for the tourists. Minorcans don't put themselves out in that way, though. Vanessa tells me that on the pleasure-boats off Majorca, they play 'Y Viva España' and have all the passengers playing castanets. We wouldn't do that here. We like things to be low-key and natural.'

'So do I. Come on, I'm starving.'

Vanessa had recommended the restaurant, too: one in the back streets of the town, quieter than the tourist traps around the harbour, that served authentic Minorcan food. They ate crisp little sardines, fried with parsley and garlic, followed by hefty steaks.

'You haven't told me yet,' Laurent said, 'how you come to be on the island.'

'Because of Juan and Sophie, basically, and because I wanted a summer job that would give me a chance to improve my languages.'

Lucy went on to tell him about her studies at the university. She was doing an international business studies course, she explained, which combined languages with accountancy and business law.

'So that's why you speak French and German so well,' Laurent said.

'And Spanish—Castilian at least, though my Catalan is still a bit rough. I have a smattering of Italian, too. I always enjoyed language studies, and my parents took me travelling a lot with them when I was younger. But I reckoned they were right when they advised me that I needed a more solid basis than linguistics for a career, and though many people seem to think accountancy is boring, I do find that part of my course interesting too.'

'So what will you do after you graduate?'

'Something like you do,' Lucy said. She watched the surprise appear in Laurent's face. It wasn't unexpected, she managed to laugh at it. 'Seriously, that is what I have in mind. I'd like to go into international finance in some capacity, and I've thought of working abroad at least for a while, in Paris or Vienna or one of the other financial centres. I'm maybe not ambitious enough to make it to the very top, but I am thinking in terms of a proper career, and once I graduate I should have qualifications good enough to get me a traineeship with a merchant bank, or something similar. In the long run, I guess I'm aiming at something very like your kind of job.'

The surprise had faded from his face, to be replaced with an expression of polite interest. He said lightly, 'I'd never have thought it, Cinderella. You're right, though; those are the kind of qualifications you need in my sort of job. And I can't deny that it's rewarding.'

'But hard work.'

'Oh, yes. There's little open prejudice against women in banking these days, but they rarely make it to board level, I think because it's so hard for them to be single-minded enough. You can't really combine a high-level career in finance with family life.'

'You did,' Lucy pointed out.

'Unsuccessfully.'

The response was so bleak that Lucy didn't like to probe too deeply. She said carefully, 'It's always hard for women these days, I think, whatever combination of career and marriage they go for. I certainly imagine that I'll marry one day, and I can't see myself being happy with a man who doesn't have a successful career of his own. But it's true, I suppose, that it's difficult too for a woman to centre her life on a man when he's preoccupied with a job that excludes her. Imagine being alone in the house all day, or with only small children for company, and then having to respond graciously when your husband rings up to say he'll be two or three hours late for dinner!'

Laurent gave a rueful smile. 'I used to do that several times a week to Catherine,' he confessed.

'Poor Catherine.'

'Oh, I saw even then how unfair it was to her. But it wasn't something I could change to suit her convenience.'

'So wouldn't there be something to be said for a wife with an absorbing career of her own?'

'There are disadvantages to that pattern, too.'

'I'm sure there are, but they can't be as bad as the disadvantages of spending a lifetime alone.'

Laurent took a sip of his coffee instead of replying, and Lucy sensed that she had taken her propaganda far enough for a first attempt. 'Anyway,' she continued, 'you're not alone, are you? There's your son. Gilles.'

'Yes, there's Gilles.'

'Do you see him often?'

'As often as I can.' He smiled again, a little sadly. 'More, in fact, than I tended to do when Catherine and I were together. Nowadays I make appointments to meet Gilles: an hour after school once a week to take him to his football practice, an outing together every alternate Sunday afternoon...'

'Perhaps you should have done that when you were married.'

'Perhaps I should. Some busy couples I know work on just such a basis, with each other and with their children. They book lunches and suppers together as much as six weeks in advance.'

Lucy laughed, as Laurent seemed to intend her to. Privately she thought how horrific that sounded. Imagine having to work to find time for one's life-partner! But it wasn't fair to scoff, she reminded herself; any couple who managed to make a success of modern marriage deserved admiration, not carping criticism of the solutions they had worked out to their problems.

She said, 'Do you have a picture of Gilles?'

That was pushing, she thought as soon as she had said it, but she couldn't help being curious about Laurent's son. And he took the question well. 'Of course,' he agreed, and reached for his wallet. He withdrew a small snapshot, and glanced affectionately at it before handing it over. 'This was taken last Christmas.'

Lucy looked. It showed a small boy with an enormous grin, holding a very impressive-looking model aeroplane. Gilles was much fairer than his father, with blue eyes instead of Laurent's brown ones, but Lucy thought she could see the resemblance between the two of them in the wide mouth and the high cheekbones. She said so to Laurent.

Laurent nodded. 'Gilles is like me in temperament, too,' he said. 'He's a thoughtful child, but he has a great capacity for pleasure. I've missed him more than I expected this last month.'

'It's a pity you couldn't bring him with you.'

'I'd not have done that in the circumstances.'

Up till then, Lucy had managed to forget about the death threats. It hurt to be reminded of them.

That kind of occurrence couldn't sit well with family life either, she thought. But it wasn't as if death threats were a regular hazard for bankers, and, though it had made sense for Laurent to keep his son away from any danger, she felt it would have been so much easier for him if he had had somebody he loved, and who loved him, to help him through that difficult time.

'Perhaps next year,' she murmured, handing back the photograph. Laurent pocketed it, and deftly brought the conversation back to shallower waters.

It was dark outside by the time they had finished their second cups of coffee and Laurent had paid the bill. As they left the restaurant he slipped his arm round Lucy's shoulders. She could feel his thigh brushing against hers as they walked along.

How lonely he must be, she thought again. Whatever he pretended, he didn't seem to her to be the kind of man who could be happy living alone, taking the edge off his appetite for love and affection with occasional short flings. 'A great capacity for pleasure,' he had said of Gilles—and, by implication, of himself. That capacity hadn't been used to the full for a long while, she sensed. He needed love in his life, even if he found it difficult to make the time for it.

At least on Minorca he had the time; at least there wasn't an office on the island, perpetually calling him away from her. On Minorca she would have a chance, Lucy thought, to claim more of his time and attention than he was likely to accord to any woman he met casually in Paris.

But she wouldn't be fixing her place in Laurent's real life, his workaday life, she would only be establishing herself as a holiday companion. Would it ever be possible to make the transition from one to the other? Would he ever look beyond Cinderella, beyond Lucy the boat guide, and start to see an intelligent, thoughtful woman who might one day share his life? For all her sincere attempts to show him the serious side of her character, she was conscious that he hadn't yet done so.

They reached his car, and got into it. It was quiet and dark in the side street; there was nobody else in sight. Laurent reached over, and took Lucy in his arms.

His kisses were feather-light, dancing around her mouth, then drifting, teasingly, to brush her cheek, her eyelashes, the short strands of hair above her ears. They were delicious, and yet frustrating. It was as if she wasn't really touching the lonely man with a deep capacity for sharing, for love; she was just flirting with a holiday-maker looking for a casual romance. Laurent's touch then seemed to her to be all technique, with no feeling behind it. He wasn't kissing the real Lucy Sanderson, he was just amusing himself with Cinderella.

This was all wrong, she thought. She didn't want him to gain the impression that she would welcome it if he took her back to his villa and went on to make love to her in this casually expert way. She sensed what would happen then: he would drop her just as casually as soon as she had filled her momentary function in his life. But at the same time she felt that he would be frightened away if she responded with too much intensity. And if she simply stopped him, he might rapidly lose the little interest he had so far showed in her, and she would have no opportunity to carve out a real place for herself in his life.

Her mind was hopelessly divided, but her body was very sure what it needed. It wanted him to go on, and on. It wanted all this and more. It had been a long time for her, too—more than a year since a man had touched her intimately. This man was so skilful, his touch such a delight, he knew just how to arouse her physical responses. His hand drifted down the curtain of her hair, then pushed it aside, and moved to caress her shoulder. His fingers, supple and experienced, seemed to trace the pattern of each nerve under her skin.

She could feel her reaction deepen, from a tingle into an ache. He sensed her growing arousal, and slipped his hand under the light material of her dress. His palm just cupped the swell of her breast. The light pressure on her nipple was tormenting; she pressed forward to increase it, but he moved as she did, circling the pink bud in a little cage of fingertips.

It was a game, and a delicious one—or would have been, if she had been confident that her longings would eventually be fulfilled. Physically, yes—oh, yes. He would rouse and rouse her till the ache became all but unbearable, and then proceed to satisfy her very thoroughly, no doubt. But would she be able to bear it if all through their lovemaking he remained what he was just then, a desirable, sophisticated stranger? Would she be able to face herself afterwards, if she gave herself to him, and was given no more than transitory physical satisfaction in return?

His mouth now was following his hand downwards, tracing a light path across her brown skin. His lips and his tongue were warm against her; the sudden touch of his teeth was cool and startling. Delicious, oh, so delicious. This wasn't what she wanted, Lucy tried to tell herself, but he was bringing her such exquisite pleasure that she couldn't bear to stop him just yet. He pulled her dress aside, and deposited light kisses all over the uppermost curves of her breast. His teeth moved to trap her nipple, and his tongue flicked at its tip until the sensation was more than an ache, it was a burning focus of longing.

Lucy couldn't restrain herself any longer. Her leg reached out in the darkness of the car, groping for and finding his, twining around it. Her hands tightened on his back, her breath began to come in short, soft pants.

Suddenly Laurent was sitting up, drawing away from her. He gently straightened Lucy's dress, and settled one last light kiss on her mouth.

'Lovely Lucy,' he said quietly, 'we'd better be on our way back.'

Lucy watched him fasten his seat-belt and fumble for the ignition key. She felt limp, drained. Heavens, she had clean forgotten that they were sitting in a car in a side street, that only the darkness afforded them any privacy at all. If he hadn't stopped them, she sensed, she wouldn't have been able to do it herself.

He switched on the cassette player, and the strains of a Mozart sonata, elegant and sophisticated, filled the car. He drove in silence, past the last houses of Ciudadela and on to the main road to Mahon.

Lucy glanced at the clock on the dashboard. They had eaten late; it was already eleven. Even if he drove straight for Villa Carlos it would be almost twelve by the time they reached Juan and Sophie's villa. He couldn't take her to his own villa and have her home by midnight as he had promised Juan. And he wouldn't make love to her in the car, she sensed; she was reprieved for the night.

The terrible thing was her disappointment at the prospect. This was dangerous, she thought helplessly. She didn't have remotely enough experience to know how to handle his sexual advances; if he made a serious attempt to seduce her she would be as good as lost. And it wasn't a question of if, surely, but of when. He was an experienced man—he might take his time, but he wouldn't be content for ever with fumbled embraces in a car. If she agreed to see him again, she would be as good as consenting to his lovemaking.

Lucy, Lucy, what do you want? she asked herself ruefully. All right, there is one very simple answer— you want this man. But do you want him on any basis on which you have the remotest realistic hope of getting him? Shouldn't you accept the fact that he is getting through to you an awful lot more rapidly than you seem to be getting through to him?

She turned to look at him. The crisp silhouette of his face was outlined against the car window. How dear he could be to her, she thought; how dear he had become already. And how much, she added to herself, he would be able to hurt her if she let herself be drawn any deeper into this relationship.

'I enjoyed the trip this afternoon,' he said suddenly. 'Perhaps I should do it again one day. Or I might come on the mystery tour with you . . .'

'I'm not sure you'd particularly enjoy the mystery tour,' Lucy said honestly. 'It's really a beach-finding excursion, designed for families as much as anything. Too much lounging around for your taste! The trip you would like, I should think, is the one on the ferry that goes to Lazareto. There's much more to see on the old quarantine island.'

'The *San Felipe* does that trip?'

'No, it's a different ferry. It's a short trip, but the ferry only goes a couple of times a week: on Fridays and Mondays, at five-thirty.'

'Would you be free in time to come on Friday?'

On Friday? That was two days off. It was just what she did want, Lucy thought suddenly, to spend some time with Laurent on a more casual basis, with other people around to ensure that, physically, things didn't move any faster than she could handle.

'I should be able to make the ferry if I run,' she said thoughtfully.

Laurent gave a short laugh. 'As I learned the hard way,' he said, 'you run pretty well.'

'We'll need to meet at Cales Fons.'

Lucy explained where the Lazareto ferry sailed from, and where Laurent could buy the tickets, ready for her headlong dash over to the bay from Cala Corb.

'I'll see you then,' Laurent said, as he pulled up the Renault outside Juan and Sophie's villa.

'You're not coming in now?'

'It's rather late, I don't think so.' He leaned over to kiss her. His lips lingered only briefly, then he reached past her to unfasten the car door. 'Sleep well.'

Friday, Lucy thought. Two days. Two whole days before she saw him again. Be grateful, Lucy, for the break, for the chance to think again before you leap into an affair with him.

As she was fitting her key into the doorlock she heard his car behind her, revving up and roaring away down the road towards Villa Carlos.

CHAPTER EIGHT

IT WAS already five-thirty-five by Lucy's watch when the *San Felipe* berthed on Friday afternoon. Juan told her, smiling, that she could leave it to him to help the passengers off, but she still had to run all the way up the steps to the Miranda, and through the town to the other harbour.

She was just in time; the Lazareto boat was still at its moorings when she arrived, panting, on the quayside. She paused for a moment, looking for Laurent, then saw him stand up inside the boat and gesture to her.

'I've saved you a space,' he said with a smile, guiding her to the wooden bench where he had been sitting.

'I thought I'd miss it for a moment.'

'So did I. The boatman promised to wait till twenty-to, but I don't think I could have held him beyond then.'

'I could have had a coffee, I guess, and waited for you at Cales Fons.'

Laurent gave her a surprised look. 'Oh, I wouldn't have gone without you.'

No, he wouldn't have done, Lucy realised, even though it was a trip he knew she had done before. She had done some hard thinking about their relationship during the previous two days. It was silly of her, she thought now, to have imagined that

Laurent wasn't really interested in her. She could see that he hadn't at all been acting like a man whose only concern was to get her to bed.

At first, she knew it had been his fear of the terrorists, his reluctance to leave the villa, that had kept him from seeing more of her. And now that the threat was lifted—now, she suspected, his motives for holding back were much the same as hers. It wasn't that he didn't desire her, she was certain that he did. It was more that he too was lonely and vulnerable. It was only too understandable that he should hesitate to throw himself into a relationship that, he might think, could only last for the short time they were on the island.

Perhaps he wouldn't try to make love to her after all. And, if he did, then it would mean—maybe not just as much to him as it would to her, but it would certainly mean something to him. It would intensify the pain of parting afterwards for him, just as it would for her. Just because he was an expert lover, she didn't have to assume that there was no feeling underlying his skilful caresses.

Perhaps the only difference was that he seemed quite convinced that they *would* part when they left the island, and Lucy wasn't. She wanted, she *needed* to feel that they might have a longer future together. She imagined that there might not be that certain pain afterwards, after all, and Laurent seemed so sure that there would be.

She hoped to convince him that he was wrong. But what if he was right? Then mightn't it make sense for her to leave it to him to set the pace of their relationship, and to decide how far it would eventually go?

He was more experienced than she, after all, not just in the superficial arts of love, but in the feelings they intensified, both good and bad.

He took her hand just then, and squeezed it. Lucy squeezed back. Trust him, she told herself. OK, he wasn't a saint, but she was willing to bet that he was a sincere, honest and thoughtful man, who would weigh her own prospects of pleasure and pain just as carefully as he weighed his own.

Soon they were out of Cala Corb, and moving across the main harbour towards the Lazareto. Lucy pointed out to Laurent the two stone lions that guarded the gate to the quarantine hospital. British lions, Juan had always insisted; Spanish lions always smiled, but these were glum ones.

'No wonder,' said Laurent. 'It can't have been much fun, being sent to the Lazareto.'

'True. So many people died of cholera and other diseases that they didn't even bury them in the cemetery. The hospital workers got private graves, but the bodies of the immigrants were just thrown into a pit. Every so often they used to excavate the bones, and heap them up against the walls.'

'I didn't know you had a gory streak,' Laurent teased.

'I don't. It's history that was gory—it's nothing in me.'

'I wouldn't be too sure. I reckon you have a vivid imagination.'

Yes, Lucy thought. Sometimes I do, all too vivid.

Though she had seen everything on the Lazareto before, she enjoyed seeing it again through Laurent's eyes. He seemed very interested in the trip, and he

asked both her and the Spanish guide a lot of questions—some of which neither of them could answer!
They saw the smoke chamber, where visitors had to
pass through a thick cloud of black smoke for fumi-
gation, the altar to Saint Sebastian, and the small
stone cells from which the inmates were allowed to
hear mass, at a safe distance from the visiting priest.
They passed through the allotments where food had
been grown to keep the island self-sufficient, and the
tiny museum with its rows of apothecary jars.

'The English abroad,' Laurent mused, as the ferry
was taking them back to Cales Fons after an all too
short trip. 'I wonder if this island would be as popular
with the British today if we hadn't possessed it two
hundred years ago?'

'*We?*' Lucy teased. 'You're not an Englishman. It's
a bit of a cheek, you talking about "us"!'

'Oh, but I am—at least, in as far as I can lay claim
to any one nationality. My mother is French, but my
father was English. I have an English surname,
Buckley, and a British passport.'

Señor Buckley, Lucy thought. She had heard the
name somewhere before, but it hadn't registered. How
very little she really knew about Laurent even now!

'I didn't even know your name,' she said
awkwardly.

'I don't know your surname either.'

'It's Sanderson. Very English.' She hesitated, then
went on. 'Have you lived all your life in France?'

'Oh, no. I grew up in England, and went to school
there, though I always spent my holidays with my
mother's family in Normandy. Then I decided to go

to university in Paris, and I met Catherine, and that decided my fate.'

'And you reckon to stay in France for ever?'

'Probably. Certainly, while Gilles is a child. I'd not be able to see him nearly as regularly if I lived anywhere else but Paris.'

'I'm sure he needs you in his life.'

'So am I,' Laurent agreed. 'And I need him too, I think.'

Those set appointments, Lucy thought, and then pushed the thought aside as unfair. Laurent couldn't help the demands of his job, and he genuinely did like children: she had seen that when he had encountered Juan and Sophie's brood.

'It's a nice age, six,' she said.

'True. Boys of six are old enough to take a sensible interest in things. Which reminds me, I'd suggested to Sophie that we might take Manuel fishing one afternoon soon.'

Had he? Lucy thought, surprised. But perhaps it wasn't so surprising, she told herself. It couldn't be easy, being a part-time father and switching on to a six-year-old's wavelength for fixed meetings only. Laurent might well see an advantage in breaking up this longish separation from Gilles by spending some time with another small boy. And he had, she thought to herself, made consistent efforts to charm Juan and Sophie ever since he had met them.

'I've only one afternoon off a week,' Lucy said. 'Tuesday. Could we make it then?'

As soon as she had said it she could have bitten her tongue. Tuesday was three days off. Would that mean that she wouldn't see Laurent over the weekend?

'Why not?' he agreed. 'I'll come back to Sophie's with you and see if that's OK with her.'

'She told me to invite you to supper tonight,' Lucy said, on the spur of the moment. Sophie almost certainly wouldn't mind, she was always excellent at feeding unexpected visitors.

'That would be nice.'

They stopped at a supermarket in Villa Carlos, and Laurent carefully chose two bottles of wine before driving Lucy over to Juan and Sophie's villa.

'Laurent said he'd love to accept your invitation and stay to supper,' Lucy said breathlessly, as soon as they were indoors.

Sophie barely raised her eyebrows. 'Fine,' she agreed.

It was a pleasant, relaxed evening. Laurent seemed to get on so well with Juan and Sophie. He had a very natural ability to adjust to the company he was with, Lucy thought to herself; she had no doubt that in Paris he would be a very typical merchant banker, at home in the stuffiest of circles, but he seemed equally at ease in the chaos of Sophie's living-room. He chatted easily with Juan and Manuel about fishing and Spanish football, he enthusiastically praised Sophie's spicy beef stew, *and* discussed the recipe with her.

Quite a range. But she herself would be able to match it, Lucy thought to herself, with a little practice. She would have to convince him of that, if they were to have any chance of building a permanent relationship: that she would fit in with his Parisian friends just as well as he blended with her Minorcan ones.

And if it meant going to bed with him without any promises for the future, in order to win herself the opportunity to show him that she could manage that, then wouldn't it be worth the risk? Knowing, as she thought she did, that he would be risking almost as much?

'I really must return the compliment,' he said, as he was shaking Sophie's hand before saying goodbye, 'and invite all of you over to my villa.'

Sophie shrugged. 'That's tricky, with the kids. Cara's at an age when I don't like to mess up her bed-times, and it takes a bit of arranging to fix a baby-sitter who can cope with getting her settled properly. Don't feel you have to ask me and Juan over when you ask Lucy. Your housekeeper would act as a chaperon, wouldn't she?'

'Juana? Yes, of course. Then you won't be of-fended, Juan, if I ask Lucy to come and dine with me tomorrow evening?'

To come and dine with him? To come alone to the villa? Even if Juana was there—in theory—then surely, Lucy thought, that must mean that he had de-cided he wanted to make love to her, whatever the pain it might eventually bring to both of them.

Juan grinned broadly. 'Not at all.'

Lucy dressed carefully for her visit to Laurent's villa. The third time she had been there, she thought to herself—and the first time she had actually been invited!

She seriously considered trying to look like a Parisian Lucy. Her holiday wardrobe didn't stretch to Chanel suits, but she would be able to look like an

efficient young lady banker if she tried, surely: put
her hair up, wear the skirt and jacket she had worn
on the plane over to the island, perhaps even dig out
a pair of tights instead of going barelegged. No, there
would be no point unless she explained why she was
doing it, and it was too soon in their relationship for
that. Better to be a casually seductive Cinderella,
happy to stake out her small place in Laurent's life,
and willing—as he seemed to be—to take her chances
on the future.

She wore the blue dress she had worn for their
dinner in Ciudadela; it was the dress she felt most
confident in. And she washed her hair just before
going out, and let it dry in the sun so that it spread
in soft waves down past her shoulders.

Juan lent her his car. She had refused Laurent's
offer to fetch and return her, and she knew that it
wouldn't be safe to come back late at night on a hired
moped or on the *Sophie*. Nor could she stay over;
Juan would have had a fit if she had suggested it!

Her spirits lifted as she drove out of Mahon and
along the road to the villa, past the Golden Farm, the
big red house where Nelson was said to have lived.
Don't take it so seriously, Lucy, she told herself, as
she sang along with the Spanish pop songs blaring
out of Juan's car radio. Enjoy tonight, it will be good.
And then, if it turns out that he's right for you, and
you are right for him, there will be nothing to worry
about. And if he's not, if you're not...at least you
will have learned something. And who knows, perhaps
you will go home with a wonderful memory to keep
you warm on the cold, empty evenings that follow.

Laurent greeted her on the doorstep, cool and re-laxed in blue denim, and led her into the kitchen.

'Juana's not here?' she asked.

He shook his head. 'Don't tell Juan, but I gave her and Alonzo the evening off. I'm doing the cooking myself.'

'Can I help?'

'No. This is my night.'

He tossed two steaks into a pan as he spoke, and while they were sizzling he rapidly sliced bread, tossed salad, and uncorked a bottle of wine. Lucy sat down at the kitchen table—already set for supper for two—and watched him, surprised and impressed by his casual confidence. The menu he had chosen wasn't elaborate, but he handled the food with easy familiarity.

He flavoured the steaks with herbs from Juana's garden. They were delicious.

'I haven't done a dessert,' he said, when they finished their main course. 'There's cheese. Or I could find some ice-cream in the freezer...'

'Cheese would be perfect,' Lucy assured him.

They lingered over the cheese, talking mainly about food, on the island and in France. Lucy had spent several hot summers in the south of France, holidaying with her parents, and she could match Laurent's reminiscences fairly well, though some of the restaurants he mentioned were known to her only by reputation.

She was used to English friends being impressed by her fluent French, but it didn't impress Laurent, she had realised by now. He spoke as many languages as she did, and he seemed to take her skills for granted.

They were so much more common, she supposed, on the European mainland than they were in England.

It was very quiet in the kitchen. There were no blinds at the wide windows, just darkness, with a faint reflection of the two of them sitting at opposite sides of the kitchen table. Every scuffle of their chairs, every clink of their knives, sounded clearly. With another man Lucy might have found the silence oppressive, but with Laurent she felt strangely at ease.

'Let's go through,' he said. She mentioned the washing up, but he told her that Juana would see to it in the morning, airily tipping their empty plates into the sink.

He led her to the sitting-room, and threw himself down, long legs splayed out, on to one of the low leather sofas.

'There should be music,' he said. 'I'm sorry, I've lived here so little. I don't have any records here, or books, or...'

Lucy thought, quite suddenly, that he had never seduced a woman in the villa before. In his Paris apartment he might have been suave and practised, knowing exactly what records to play, where to sit, how best to guide her through to his bedroom, but here he would have to ad lib as the evening progressed. All through their brief relationship he had treated her as a very special individual; it was nice to think that this would continue, that at this vital moment there was no danger of his slipping into a standard seduction routine. The thought brought a smile to her face.

'What's so funny?'

She considered what to tell him.

'I was just wondering what music you would have chosen to play.'

'Oh, Mozart, of course,' he said airily, getting to his feet. 'Subtle but insistent.'

He reached out and took her hand, and, as she did so, let his eyes connect with hers. Electric awareness flowed through Lucy like a current. I want him so much, she thought. This really is what I want, even if, in the end, it turns out that I only have him for tonight.

His lips just brushed the pulse of her inside wrist, then his fingers parted hers, and a tantalising tongue circled round her palm, sending a hot thrill right through her body. Slowly, slowly, he let his mouth travel up her arm. He lingered at the crook of her elbow, sensing the points where she was most responsive, probing and teasing until Lucy felt her legs would give way under her.

When his mouth reached the base of her neck, he moved forward to take her in his arms. Her legs did fail her then, and she let him take her weight, glorying in the strength and sureness of his slim, muscular body.

Already she was overwhelmed, and he hadn't even begun to undress her. He picked her up bodily, and carried her across to one of the sofas, straightening himself when he had gently deposited her, and standing there for a moment, looking down on her.

'Lucy, Lucy,' he whispered. He knelt down beside her, and began to undo the buttons that ran down the front of her blue dress. When he came to the tie belt at her waist, he unfastened that too. He didn't stop until he reached the hem. Then he folded the dress back. Underneath it, Lucy was wearing only a tiny pair of lacy panties.

She had forgotten how tiny they were, until she felt his eyes on her. His gaze raked down her, and then up, and down again. His eyes seemed to linger on her bare breasts, and they tingled as if he was already touching them.

He didn't touch them. He simply looked at her, in the quiet, still room, until she began to quiver with anticipation. Her breathing sounded loud and ragged to her.

'Laurent.'

It was a plea. And, meeting her eyes, he laughed silently, as if he was enjoying his power over her, enjoying this special and serious game of man and woman. Then he moved, taking her by the arm again, and pulling her to the floor next to him. He kissed her on the mouth, long, sweetly, as his expert fingers slipped the dress from her shoulders, leaving her all but naked in his arms.

Lucy tried to press against him, longing to feel even the material of his shirt against her aching breasts. But he slid his hands between their bodies, guiding her away, denying her even this little satisfaction.

'Gently,' he said. His mouth drifted down her body, exploring her skin, each touch tantalisingly light, until he lingered, pressing tiny kisses on the white strip of skin above her panties. Her body burned. She wanted to writhe and thrash against him, but his hands, firm on her waist and thigh, held her prisoner.

The ache was inside her now, deep inside. She fought to still it, and as she began to relax beneath him, he moved his mouth upwards again. His tongue circled round the peak of her breast, turning her nipple to a throbbing core of awareness. He trapped it lightly between his teeth, and Lucy let out a groan.

'Gently,' he said again, and brought his mouth back to hers. His kiss was still deliberately light, his tongue elusive as she snaked her own between his parted lips. His hands found her breasts now, and he rubbed her nipples gently between his thumbs and forefingers. Lucy, breaking free from his kiss, tried to reach for the belt of his trousers. His hand caught hers as it touched the buckle. He brought it up between them.

'You do want me?' he asked, suddenly intent. 'You're sure?'

'Yes. Oh, yes.' Lucy's hips moved hungrily towards his, but he eluded her again, slipping to his feet, and pulling her after him.

'Not here.'

He picked her up bodily, shifting her weight in his arms, and strode easily along a stepped corridor down which Lucy had not yet ventured.

She hardly noticed his room, simply that there was a bed, wide, surprisingly hard by Minorcan standards, with a cool white-covered quilt. He deposited her gently on it, and then straightened up and began to take off his clothes, with as much unhurried ease as if he had been alone.

Lucy watched him. His tan was deeper than hers, his body powerful and yet economically built, its lines lean and efficient. She was longing to reach out and touch him, but she sensed that he would not like that: this was his game, he was setting the rules. He peeled down his denims and then stripped off his briefs, seemingly quite unembarrassed about his arousal. He was aroused, very aroused.

Laurent moved to kneel on the bed, astride her, their bodies everywhere a little apart.

'Touch me,' he said.

Her turn. Not to abandon herself, not yet, but to display a control and finesse as nearly equal to his as she could manage. She brought her arms up to clasp behind his shoulders, and arched her body upwards until her breasts just brushed against his bare chest. Moving against him brought her such exquisite pleasure that she almost forgot she was trying to pleasure him. He laughed into her eyes, and bent to kiss her, before rolling over on to his back, and pulling her gently towards him.

She used her hands this time, and her mouth, as he had done, touching him everywhere but where he most wanted to be touched, trying to sense from his smallest responses where his nerve-endings lay, where his reactions would be strongest. He let her do just as she chose until she moved to bring his hard thigh between hers, and then he eased her away, denying her any chance to satisfy the ever-growing ache inside her.

His mouth moved again to her breast, and he sucked gently at it, intensifying her desire to a point she would not have believed possible. Her own control was fading again, but his seemed as solid as ever. He was experienced enough, she felt sure, to judge its breaking point to perfection. Only the certainty that he would eventually fulfil her totally made it possible to endure the exquisite agony.

No more, though, no more. Her body, frantic now, pleaded with him for release. He moved her gently on to her back, and reached to ease down the tiny scrap of lace that still covered her.

He replaced it with his mouth, tracing delicate patterns with his tongue and lips on the sensitive skin of her groin and upper thigh. Lucy groaned, blind now to everything but the longing to feel him inside her.

He moved upwards, and thrust, filling her at last. Even as her response built around him, though, he was withdrawing again. Her body seemed to clutch and spasm in still-frustrated longing. He judged the very instant when the spasm faded, and thrust again, withdrew again before he had given her time for her body to react.

Lucy grabbed at him, her nails raking his shoulders, desperate to end the game. He was not laughing now; there was a thin film of sweat on his face and body, and her hands slithered against it.

She knew the very instant when his control left him, sensed almost before he did the time when he would be unable to withdraw. Her body seemed to explode around him, the waves of delight pulsing through her, the hot blood rushing to her skin, bringing out a flush all over her. As the wave subsided he began to move in her, rhythmically, easily, his body asserting its total possession of hers. Then he too cried out, and she felt the deep spasms of his final release.

Afterwards they lay exhausted, both of them soaked in sweat, the bed a tangle of damp sheets around them. The blood still seemed to hammer in Lucy's head. She was still too shattered to think, to take in anything but the amazing knowledge of her body's reactions. Had she been a totally inexperienced virgin, the depth of her responses could not have astonished her more.

Laurent moved first, swinging his feet to the floor, and swivelling round to look at her.

'Come and swim,' he said.

Lucy looked back at him. She still felt beyond speech. And there was no need to tell him how wonderful it had been—he knew, every movement of her body had told him so.

He stood up and crossed the room. It had sliding glass doors, Lucy now saw, that led on to the courtyard. He opened them, slipped out, and a moment later a warm pool of light flooded the yard.

It was a moment after she had heard the splash of his body hitting the water before she could bring herself to move. She padded to the door, still naked, and went to the edge of the pool. He was swimming underwater, the dark shape of his body obscured by the reflection of the floodlight on the surface.

He surfaced suddenly, and tossed his head to shake off the water. 'Want me to pull you in?'

She reckoned he might, at that. She took a deep breath and dived, cutting the water a couple of feet from where he waited for her.

It was colder than she had expected; he might have warned her of that, she thought, as she resurfaced. He stood still for a moment, letting her regain her breath, then set off after her, in a long, loping, expert crawl.

She wasn't sure if he expected her to move, but she did, slipping past him before he could sense her position and change direction. Lucy was a good swimmer, but Laurent was a better one, she realised. His fast, economical stroke was no great advantage in the small pool, though, and by dipping and weaving, above and below the surface, she managed to elude him for several minutes before he finally trapped her in a corner.

His legs and arms were splayed across the corner, penning her in, and she had not the breath left to dive past him. Half panting, half laughing, she met his look, and his mouth descended on hers, his breath still quick and shallow, mingling with her own. His body was cool now to the touch, and still slightly slippery.

'The pool won't wash the sweat off,' he said. 'We'll shower in a moment.'

Not yet. She wanted to stand there with him in the darkness, feeling the water lap around them where their chase had disturbed it, feeling his arms enfolding her and his breath warm against her neck. His lips just touched her, surprisingly cool, his tongue between them surprisingly warm.

'Mmmm,' Lucy sighed. A different man might have taken advantage of the quiet moment to tell her that he loved her, but not this one, she told herself. He had given her so much more than she had expected, but even now he would try to hold back his heart. Even now he believed that they would part before long. At least he wouldn't lie to her. He hadn't seduced her with false promises or worthless words of love; she had come to him willingly, because even on these terms she had wanted it all to happen.

'Come on,' Laurent said. 'I'll soap you under the shower.'

His bathroom was the twin of the one she had used before, white-tiled, clinically efficient. The hot water steamed off their bodies; his soap, pine-scented, stung her nostrils. He lathered her all over, his hands moving steadily over her body, and she lathered him, still astonished at the knowledge of what his body could do to hers.

She had felt so drained, half an hour earlier, that she would not have believed she could want him again so soon, or that he would expect to make love to her once more. But she could; he did.

CHAPTER NINE

'WHERE do we go?' Laurent asked.

'I thought we'd walk out past Cala Pedrera,' Lucy told him. 'That's the bay just beyond the town, where we took the boat on the harbour trip. We can walk out towards the sea there, over the fields, and collect some snails, and then come down to the bay to fish afterwards.'

'Sounds good.'

It was four o'clock. The sun was just beginning to drop, and Villa Carlos was slowly waking up after its siesta. Lucy and Laurent had been lazing around Sophie and Juan's villa since lunch time, and now Manuel was impatient for them to set off with him on the promised fishing trip.

The three of them, Lucy, Laurent and Manuel, walked down towards Cala Pedrera. The road dipped and thinned into a dusty track at the head of the bay, and then revived again as it skirted a big modern development of holiday flats.

'Cannon,' said Manuel.

'Cannon? Oh, yes, on the street sign,' Laurent said, following the small boy's gaze.

'Manuel loves those cannon,' said Lucy. 'He always stops to trace the pictures.'

The roads all had street names on tiles, set into blocks of concrete at each corner, and the one at which

Manuel had paused was ornamented with little drawings of cannon.

'Carrer Lepanto,' Laurent read off the sign. 'You'll have to refresh my memory. Lepanto was a battle, wasn't it?'

'That's right, a very famous one. It was the last sea battle fought with galleys, over four hundred years ago.'

'In Mahon harbour?'

'No. I thought that, when I first saw the signs, but I looked it up in the library, and discovered that Lepanto was fought well to the east, off the coast of Greece. But it was important to Minorca because it saved this and the other Balearic Islands from invasion by the Turks.'

'So it was nothing to do with the fortifications round the harbour mouth?'

'No, nothing,' Lucy replied. 'You've seen the fortifications? St Philip's fort?'

'Only from the water,' Laurent said.

'We'll walk that way, then. If we go to the end of this road, and through the fields there, we can get to the ruins. Manuel's seen them before, of course, but it's still interesting to him. The *San Felipe* is called after the fort, and that gives him a special reason to feel connected to it. There's not much to see now, but you can climb to the top, and look out at where the ships sailed in to attack Mahon.'

'Boom boom!' went Manuel, miming the action of two cannon. Lucy laughed and took his hand, urging him on along the hot, dusty road.

'Sophie doesn't mind him playing with guns?' Laurent asked, when the boy had broken free once more and run on ahead of them.

'She won't give him toy ones. But you know, if you stop small boys playing with toy guns and bows and arrows and the rest, they'll still make-believe with any spare stick they come across.'

'I thought it was just Gilles who did that,' Laurent said.

'Oh, no. If Gilles does it, then he's very normal.'

Carrer Lepanto led on to another road bordered by a stone wall. They walked along to a low spot in the wall, clambered over, and followed a rough footpath over the rocky ground near the water's edge.

All along the shores of Mahon harbour there had been fortifications. There still were; the barracks in Villa Carlos were as busy as they had been two hundred years before, and just beyond the old fort was the start of a modern military zone. The fort itself, though, had been dismantled, and there was nothing to be seen but ruins: heavy stone walls and gun emplacements reinforcing the rock of the cliff, the outline of the star-shaped fortifications, ditches, and a few stone cellars still standing, part filled with rubbish.

Manuel ran up to the top of the hill that had held the fort; Lucy and Laurent followed more slowly.

'Do you come here often?' Laurent asked.

'I've only been here once. But I know the view from the harbour, of course. And you know most of it, don't you?'

They gazed together at the far shore with its yachts and villas; the Lazareto; the other little island that the English had called Bloody Island; and the modern defences maintained by the Spanish Navy. Then they turned to the boy. Manuel was busily planning a defence of the fort against a bombardment by sea, and Laurent soon joined in, discussing where they should place their cannon, and how they should fight back.

Lucy leaned against a stretch of stone wall, and watched the man with the young boy. It was strange, she thought, the three of them were almost a replica of the family Laurent had lost. A man and woman and a six-year-old boy. It pleased her to think that it had been Laurent's idea for the three of them to come on this outing together.

It must have hurt him so much, the divorce. To have his wife desert him, to all but lose his little son, and then to endure a summer with the constant threat of assassination hanging over him. No wonder he had retreated into a shell, behind a barricade of politeness. But she had broken through now, she sensed. Laurent wasn't hiding from her any more. And sprawling on the grass with Manuel, playing unselfconsciously, he seemed so happy and relaxed, totally different from the edgy man she had first met in Mal's bar.

This was what he had needed, she thought: a long holiday, after too many years of working through his vacations. The peace of Minorca, to set against the frantic pace of life in Paris. Friends and a lover with whom he could relax and be himself.

He glanced up at her then, and their eyes met. Lucy gave a broad smile, and after a second Laurent smiled back. He said something to Manuel, then stood up and came to join her.

'You're not bored?'

'No, not at all.'

'Tell me when you want to go.'

He went back to the game. Lucy watched. She wasn't bored, she liked watching him, she liked watching Manuel. It was less unbearably hot than it had been earlier, and there was a hint of a wind off the sea.

Manuel was the first to grow bored, abruptly, with a six-year-old's sudden loss of interest. 'Come on,' Lucy said. 'It's time for the snail hunt.'

All along the track through the field between the fort and the road there were thistle bushes. Manuel eagerly showed Laurent the greyish-brown snails that clustered on every stem of the bushes. The two of them vied with each other to see who could pop the most snails into the plastic bag Lucy had brought. In ten minutes it was full, with Manuel marginally the winner, and they were walking slowly back to the bay.

'Where do we fish?' Laurent asked.

'Near the end of the bay. Lots of the best places for fishing are high up on the cliffs, but I don't like to take Manuel there. He's a good swimmer, but he can be a bit reckless when he gets excited, and it's quite a drop to the water.'

They clambered round the end of the bay, and across a patch of low rocks, stopping on a broad rock that was dry enough for them to sit, and within casting distance of fairly deep water.

Manuel was neat with his fingers, and plenty of fishing sessions with Juan had taught him all the basics of fishing off the rocks. He and Laurent teased each other for a few minutes, thinking up wilder and wilder ideas for catching fish more quickly. None of them were remotely practicable, but in fact the water of the bay was teeming with small fish, and Lucy was confident that they would manage to land three or four before the boy grew restless.

She was right. With three rods set, they soon managed to slip four small fish into their bucket. One of them jumped straight out again, and Manuel chased it around the rocks, laughing, until Lucy caught it in her hands just before it flipped away into the sea.

After a while Manuel dropped his rod, and sat watching the fish swim around in the bucket. Lucy fell into a happy daze, semi-conscious of the boy crouched next to the bucket on the rocks behind her, of Laurent recasting his rod at her side, and of her own gently bobbing float.

A cloud floated across the sun, and Lucy, with a hint of a shiver, checked her watch. It was close to supper time.

'Time to be getting back,' she announced reluctantly.

'My job to carry the bucket,' Manuel crowed.

'We'll have to empty it.'

'But I want to show Mum my fishes!'

'Can't he?' Laurent pleaded.

Lucy shook her head firmly. 'Sorry, she said, 'but with me you have to keep fishermen's rules. And that means throwing the catch back unless you're going to eat it. We can't eat these, they are tiny and full of bones. So back they go, and no exceptions.'

'We could carry the fish home in the bucket, and then put them back in the sea later,' Manuel suggested.

'Your daddy doesn't let you do that, does he, Manuel? And do you know why? Because the fish would die. It's too hot for them in the bucket, and they are already finding it hard to breathe. See, the little rainbow fish is barely moving. It'll revive if we throw it back now, but it won't survive another hour of rocking and splashing about in a few inches of water.'

Manuel dipped in a finger, and nudged the rainbow fish. It flipped its tail limply.

'Careful,' Lucy said, as he picked up the little fish and brought it out on his palm.

'So shiny.'

'So beautiful. Too beautiful to die. Don't throw it, just slip it in the shallows. That's right.'

They tipped back all four fish, and stood watching until the last one had revived and swum away from the shore.

'Come on,' Laurent said. 'I'll buy us ice-creams in the supermarket at the edge of the town, it's so hot still, and you've been such a good boy.'

He kept to his promise even when Manuel opted for a spaceship ice lolly in a disgusting shade of purple, and to Lucy's real admiration he chose the same one for himself. When Manuel's feet began to drag on the walk back to the villa, Laurent started to sing 'The Grand Old Duke of York', and Lucy, laughing, joined in. They worked through 'Humpty Dumpty' and 'Hickory Dickory Dock' and 'Once I caught a fish alive' and half a dozen more, to the startled amusement of the tourists they passed on the road.

Manuel rushed off down the path of the villa as soon as they reached the gate, towards Sophie and

Cara on the veranda. Lucy paused, and turned to Laurent.

'I must go back now,' he said. 'I've some phone calls to make. Shall I come here for you later, or to Mal's?'

'I ought to call in on Vanessa. So I'll see you at Mal's, maybe with her as well. Around nine-thirty?'

'Or sooner.' He bent his head, kissed her lightly, and strode off towards his car.

Lucy left the villa at eight-thirty, and made her way to Vanessa's room at the Don Carlos.

'Stranger!' Vanessa exclaimed, opening the door straight after her first tentative knock.

Lucy smiled, half apologetically. It was true, she hadn't seen Vanessa for ages.

'How was Palma?'

'Hot and crowded. We had a great time. You should have come.'

'I've been having a pretty good time here.'

Vanessa's big blue eyes narrowed. 'Laurent?'

'How did you guess?'

'To be honest, Mal said something to me. It's doing you good, Lucy. You're looking positively radiant.'

'It's not doing my course work any good. I've not opened a book in days. I'll have to have the most almighty blitz on it when I get back to London.'

'Take your mind off your broken heart.'

'Something like that.'

Vanessa ran a quick comb through her red curls, and reached for her bag. 'At least you've no illusions, then. About it lasting.'

'Oh, the odd wishful thought,' Lucy said lightly. 'But no, no illusions. I said I'd meet him in Mal's.'

'I've just got to check with reception, and I'll be ready.'

Vanessa whisked herself off through the crowd of holiday-makers in the foyer, and Lucy stood waiting for her as she chatted animatedly to the girls behind the reception desk.

How down-to-earth Vanessa was, she thought affectionately. Vanessa wasn't catty, and seemed genuinely pleased at her own happiness. And she was right, of course: it wasn't any good to hold on to illusions. Lucy tried not to spend too much time daydreaming about a possible future with Laurent in Paris. Laurent had given her no indication that he thought about anything of the kind, and reluctantly she admitted to herself that it wasn't a practicable idea. Reality was going to be London, the university, a rainy autumn and that pile of work to catch up.

And no Laurent. Hadn't she always known that, deep down? Perhaps a part of her had, but another part just couldn't believe it was true. Laurent had come to mean so much to her, so quickly, she didn't know how she would be able to bear the pain, when— if—it came to parting from him.

Oh, well, she thought to herself, as she watched Vanessa deftly sidestepping a couple of awkward clients, and making her way back to her side, she had always known, too, that this was a deep-water harbour. And in the end that hadn't stopped her from diving in.

*   *   *

The next ten days were glorious. One morning they went scuba-diving, taking the power-boat out to the Illa de l'Aire, just off Punta Prima beach, on the southern shore of the island, and diving from it into the deep, clear waters of the Mediterranean. Lucy knew the best places to dive, and led Laurent to them; he proved to be the more experienced diver, and he patiently helped her to improve her technique so that she could dive deeper and see more underwater.

They fished together more seriously on another of Lucy's free mornings, taking the *Santa Caterina* out into the deep water beyond the harbour mouth. On Lucy's next day off they went to visit the monastery at Monte Toro, and had a picnic lunch in a quiet cove to the north of the island. Almost every evening they went out together, to restaurants and bars—alone sometimes, sometimes with Sophie and Juan, or with Vanessa and her friends. And at the end of every evening they would make love—sometimes at Laurent's villa, sometimes in his car, several times in the open air, in secluded spots where they could be certain of not being disturbed. Every time it was different; every time it was wonderful.

Every day, the sun shone. The *San Felipe* toured the harbour each afternoon; Lucy was brown and holiday-happy and glowing each day in the aftermath of Laurent's lovemaking. Then, inevitably, a morning came when she woke to grey skies.

There was a thin layer of cloud, sheeting the sky, hiding the sun. Not thick, not raincloud—yet—but not evaporating either, as the sun rose higher.

Sophie, over breakfast, was philosophical about it.

'Well,' she said, 'it *is* September. You must have noticed the change in the tourists on the boat. All those noisy English children are back at school. It's all couples now, and toddlers.'

'I hadn't really thought about it.'

'I wonder why not?' Sophie teased. 'Come on, Cara, eat your bread and honey. When's Laurent going back?'

'Back to Paris?' A little cold weight seemed to settle in Lucy's stomach. 'I haven't asked him.' It had been a sort of unspoken agreement between them, that they wouldn't mar this perfect time by looking forward to a much more imperfect future.

'He can hardly be staying much longer,' Sophie said. 'He must have been here well over a month already.'

Lucy thought. It was a good five weeks since she had first seen him in Mal's bar.

'The summer isn't over yet.'

'It might be sunny again tomorrow, true. But the weather always takes a turn for the worse around late September or early October. The season's over by the end of October, you know that.'

Lucy knew. Mal and Vanessa were talking already about their plans for the winter. Most of the hotels and apartments closed by mid-October, most of the bars and restaurants. She pushed back her chair from the kitchen table, not noticing its protesting scrape on the tiled floor.

'Have you made any plans for the morning?' Sophie asked.

They rarely made any plans in advance. It was part of the holiday style, almost everything was decided on the spur of the moment. Laurent hadn't said he would come over to Cala Corb, so he would expect her to go to the villa. She hadn't thought beyond that.

'Nothing special. I'll see Juan at the harbour around twelve.'

'It might be quite busy on the boat today. No sunbathing, you see; the tourists look for something else to keep them busy.'

'I won't be late.' A faint trace of ill temper crept into Lucy's voice.

She took the *Sophie* over to the villa. It had taken her a while to let the memory of the gun fade, and to feel comfortable walking unannounced up the steps from the quay, but now she felt perfectly at home at the villa, and even Alonzo managed an occasional nod in her direction. She moored the boat herself. It seemed harder work than usual, though she had done it unaided often before, and she kept glancing up the steps to see if Laurent would run down to help her. He didn't.

She saw him when she reached the courtyard. He was indoors, talking on the telephone, his hand waving in the air for emphasis, his back turned to her. She slipped on to one of the white-painted wooden chairs, and picked up a local paper from the flagstones. Alonzo brought Laurent a pile of papers every morning: a Barcelona daily, the Paris and London financial press, two days old.

She was on to the sports pages before the door opened, and Laurent stepped out.

'Juana told me you were here,' he said. 'I didn't hear you come.'

'You were on the phone, so I thought I'd better not disturb you.'

'Yes, something's come up.' Laurent ran a hand through his hair, every inch the tense businessman. 'I'm sorry, Lucy, but I'll be busy most of this morning, I reckon. I hope I'll be through by lunch time.'

'I promised to get back to Cala Corb by twelve.'

He shrugged. 'I'm sorry. Did you bring a book over to read?'

'No. No, I didn't, not today.'

'Well, stay around if you want to use the pool or anything.' He strode across the flagstones and gave her a rather perfunctory kiss, before turning back to the villa. He drew the door shut behind him.

Lucy sat for a moment, looking after him, the local paper folded forgotten on her lap. Through the glass door she could see Laurent, telephone receiver in one hand, reaching for his computer with the other.

She ought to go, she thought. It was nice of him to offer to let her stay, but there wasn't any reason to hang around if he was going to be busy all morning. She didn't like the thought of swimming alone in the pool, glancing up every so often to see him oblivious of her on the other side of the glass. There was nothing else for her to do in the villa.

What did she usually do with her mornings? How had she filled them before she met Laurent? She really couldn't remember. Momentarily, it seemed as if there was nothing at all to do around Mahon harbour. She threw the paper back on to the pile with a grumpy little swipe of her arm, and stood up.

Perhaps she should be working too. There was that pile of unread course books, sitting accusingly on her dressing table back at Sophie's. Somehow she wasn't in the frame of mind to go and attack them.

Instead she wandered out of the courtyard and into the villa grounds, aimlessly. She could have sunbathed on the terrace if the sun had been shining—but it wasn't. It wasn't a bad morning for fishing. She didn't feel like fishing.

The rain started when she reached the terrace. A few drops, surprising in the way raindrops were after a drought, splashing on to her head and bare arms, and then a sudden downpour, sweeping out of the sky. Lucy did the only sensible thing, which was to turn and run back to the villa. She dashed for the door to Laurent's room, and collapsed against the inside of the glass, panting.

She had deliberately not run for the living-room, but Laurent appeared at the inner bedroom door a moment later.

'I wondered if you were caught in the downpour,' he said. 'Oh, you *were* caught.' He looked her over, taking in her sopping shorts and T-shirt.

'I'll have to take these off,' Lucy said, fingering the damp fabric. 'Sorry to be a nuisance.'

'Can't be helped.' Laurent crossed to a chest of drawers. 'You'd better borrow some of my clothes.' He pulled out a pair of his shorts, and eyed them critically. 'Do you think you could wear these?'

'I guess so, just to get back to Sophie's.' She went to take them from him. He grinned at her, disconcertingly, and a hefty chunk of her annoyance evaporated. Then he rummaged again, and fished out a blue T-shirt.

'I'll come and claim them back this evening,' he said, as she was dressing in his clothes.

'You'll come to Sophie's for supper?'

'No, I wanted to take you somewhere special tonight.' He smiled again, his eyes darkening as they met hers. 'I'll come for you around eight. OK?'

'Fine.' On impulse, she pulled him down to her and kissed him. He slipped his arms round her, and held her for a moment. When they drew apart, she saw the imprint of her damp clothes on his white shirt and pale trousers.

'Take a shower before you go,' he said. 'I'll be back in the living-room, but there's no need to say goodbye. I'll see you tonight.'

That meant, 'don't bother me again', but Lucy was sufficiently appeased not to mind. She showered slowly, since she would have to wait until the rain stopped, and put on Laurent's dry clothes. The shorts fitted her surprisingly well. He has slim hips, she thought. A long back, and a nice neat bottom, smaller than hers.

The rain was almost over by the time she returned to his bedroom. She folded her own wet clothes into a bundle, and set off with no more than a glance at Laurent.

To her annoyance, she saw when she reached the last turn in the steps that Alonzo was on the quay. Laurent's clothes were perfectly decent on her, but she felt self-conscious, and she waited a moment until Alonzo disappeared out of sight before descending to the quay.

He had obviously been working on the engine of the speed-boat: pieces of it were spread out along the wood of the quay, mingled with rags, a can of oil, and various tools. The door to the boathouse was open, Lucy saw, and Alonzo had retreated inside, presumably to find another tool.

He emerged, spanner in hand, before she had untied the *Sophie*, and nodded at her.

'The *Santa Caterina* isn't working?' she asked.

Alonzo mumbled something in Catalan that she didn't follow; then, seeing her puzzlement, stepped a few paces nearer.

'I clean the boat, ready for the winter,' he said, slowly and clearly. 'Señor Buckley, he goes tomorrow. I oil the engine to stop the rust.'

Señor Buckley goes tomorrow? *Tomorrow?* Lucy couldn't find the words to answer him. She gave a sort of strangled yelp and a nod, and Alonzo, nodding again too, went back to his work.

Lucy didn't let herself think again till she was out in mid-channel. She cut the *Sophie*'s engine, then realised that the main channel of the harbour was far too busy for her to stop there, and restarted it, taking the dinghy close to the rocks just to the north of Cala Corb.

She should have been anticipating it. Everything, all morning, had been conspiring to tell her. But tomorrow? He was going back to Paris tomorrow? She hadn't faced up to the fact that the inevitable was going to happen quite so soon.

At least, she told herself, she had been given warning. Laurent clearly hadn't meant to tell her he was leaving until the last minute. Perhaps he hadn't meant to tell her even then. One last perfect evening, and then—nothing?

Face it, Lucy, she thought brutally, that's how it's going to be. It wouldn't work, with you at university in London and Laurent in Paris. Your lives would be too different, the distance would be too great. Maybe you thought you could imagine a future beyond that, a future after you graduate, when the gap between the two of you might narrow, but it's too much, to face a year's separation on the strength of a short holiday romance. Enjoy this last evening, and let him go.

She told herself that repeatedly, all the way back to Cala Corb. But all the same it was a very subdued Lucy who started to get ready for the afternoon trip round the harbour. She glanced across at Laurent's boathouse when the *San Felipe* passed it, and saw that the doors were shut and padlocked, and that the white power-boat was no longer moored at the quay.

Laurent brought flowers when he arrived at Sophie's villa that evening. Two bunches, one for Sophie and one for Lucy. Little Maria protested that there were none for her, and he gallantly plucked a rosebud from each bunch, and presented them to her with a bow.

How charming, Lucy thought, but at the same time she sensed that beneath the gallantry Laurent was withdrawn, abstracted. She wondered if the business problem that had occupied him that morning was still on his mind, but she didn't like to ask him about it.

'I want you all to myself tonight,' he said. 'I've booked at the Barcelona Grill, if that's all right with you?'

It was a predictable choice: the best known, and probably the most expensive, restaurant on the island. 'Yes, fine,' Lucy said.

They drove into Mahon in silence. Laurent parked his car, and took Lucy's arm as they walked the few yards to the restaurant.

She had never been there before. It was decorated in the dark style that in Spain was synonymous with expense: heavy oak panelling, high-backed chairs with red velvet seats, candlelight. It was still early, and there were only a scattering of people in the restaurant. They were shown to a corner table.

Laurent ordered champagne. He waited for the waiter to pour it, and raised his glass to hers.

'To happy holidays.'

'Happy holidays,' Lucy echoed. Enjoy it, Lucy, she tried to tell herself, but the leaden weight in her stomach wouldn't go away.

Laurent said gently, 'This has been such a special holiday for me, Lucy. I've rarely felt as low as I did when I had to leave Paris last month, and yet these last few weeks have been among the happiest in my life. That's all thanks to you.'

'I've felt the same.'

'I wish it didn't have to end, but this has already been the longest holiday I've taken in—heavens, ten, twelve years. I'd originally planned to go back to Paris a week ago, but I just couldn't bring myself to leave. I can't put it off any longer. I think you've already guessed that this will be our last evening. I fly out at eleven tomorrow.'

'The end of the summer,' Lucy whispered.

'It has to be,' Laurent said gently. 'But it's been a very good summer, and it will leave me with some very happy memories.'

Happy memories. She loved this man so much, he had seemed so perfect for her, and by the next morning that was all it was going to be: a happy memory. Lucy wanted to scream and shout, to tell him she couldn't bear it, to get down on her knees and beg him to write to her, to phone her, to somehow, somehow keep open the prospect of a future together.

She raised her glass once more to his.

'Happy memories,' she echoed dutifully.

CHAPTER TEN

'Oh, Lucy,' Jeannette said one morning in the Ladies on the fourth floor of Brown and Lefèvre, 'you haven't met Martine before, have you?'

Jeannette was the secretary to Lucy's group of graduate trainees. Lucy didn't recognise the dark-haired girl who was with her: another secretary, she assumed, from somewhere else in the building.

'I don't think so,' she agreed, and held out a hand. 'Lucy Sanderson.'

'Martine Lemoine.'

'Martine works as a secretary on the top floor,' Jeannette explained. 'She's so lucky, she has the most incredibly handsome boss, and divorced at that.'

'That's hardly lucky, when I'm newly married,' laughed Martine.

'Well, it makes us jealous,' Jeannette went on, unperturbed. 'I've been making eyes at him for years, but I've never had any luck catching his attention. Maybe Lucy would do better.'

'I didn't know there were any incredibly handsome men at Brown and Lefèvre,' Lucy said lightly. 'I thought Arnaud was pretty typical.'

Arnaud was the trainee with the desk next to hers: a lanky lad with horn-rimmed glasses. 'Oh, no,' said Martine. 'That only proves that you haven't seen Monsieur Buckley.'

Monsieur Buckley. For six weeks Lucy had been working at Brown and Lefèvre, and this was the first time anyone had mentioned Monsieur Buckley to her. She wouldn't have believed he was even working in the same building if she hadn't seen his name on the internal telephone list.

But hadn't she been prepared for this, ever since she had come to the Paris office for her first interview with the merchant bank she knew he worked for? Hadn't she known that she would hear of him eventually? That sooner or later she was even going to run into him? Hadn't she told herself how little it mattered, how easily she was going to be able to handle it? After all, what had Monsieur Buckley been to her, or she to him? It had been a brief holiday romance, that was all, and it had all ended more than a year before.

'I guess I haven't,' she said in a reasonably even voice.

'We'll have to engineer a meeting,' Jeannette said.

'Oh, no!'

Lucy could have bitten her tongue afterwards, but she hadn't been able to prevent the exclamation from escaping.

'No?' Martine raised her elegantly arched eyebrows. 'We'll be very subtle, I promise you.'

Lucy forced out a smile. 'Naturally you would. But I . . . I already have a boyfriend.'

'You do?' Jeannette murmured, in tones of growing interest. Then she frowned. 'You don't mean Arnaud?'

'Of course not. He's—er—a journalist on *Paris Match*.'

'Lucy! Keeping that from us!' teased Jeannette, an inveterate gossip. 'Mind, I bet Monsïeur Buckley is nicer. And richer. But wasn't there a rumour, Martine, that he was dating Michelle Lebrun?'

Michelle Lebrun! The actress? Lucy fought to quell the nasty churning in her stomach, and to keep her expression of polite interest steady on her face.

She couldn't help feeling relieved, though, when Martine responded with a little shake of the head.

'There was a piece in the gossip columns a while back, but believe me, it's not true. That man never seems to talk on the phone to any woman, except very occasionally to his ex-wife. And he works so late each evening that I really can't believe his love-life is all it's reputed to be.'

'What a waste,' Jeannette mourned.

'True. It might improve his temper if only he had a girlfriend. He used to be such a charming man, but for the last year or so he's had a real tendency to fly off the handle whenever I make a mistake in his letters...'

Lucy forced herself to linger for a few minutes more, until the girls had gone on to discuss other men in the office. Then she snapped her handbag shut on her mirror and lipstick, and quietly moved away.

Don't think about it, she told herself, as she got back to the desk next to Arnaud. Think about the journalist on *Paris Match*. What was his name? Jean, wasn't it? You'd better give him a ring, Lucy, and tell him that if the offer's still open, you'd love to go to that concert with him on Friday, after all.

That day seemed endless. It was a relief to Lucy when she finally got back to her little one-and-a-half room apartment in a scruffy street behind the Gare Montparnasse. She went straight to the kitchenette and made herself a strong cup of black coffee. Then she sat down on the divan, and drank it slowly.

She glanced around her. The apartment was cramped, and most of the furniture was old and scratched, but she had worked hard at making it cosy. Impressionist prints brightened the walls, there were pot plants on the windowsill, and she had splashed out some of her first paypacket on a gay stripy cover for the divan.

What was Laurent's Paris house like? she wondered. Not much like this, she was willing to bet. There was still a vast gulf dividing his life and hers.

But she hadn't come to Paris to find Laurent Buckley again, had she? That was over, completely over, and it was only her own idiotic stubbornness that kept her from forgetting him. She had come to Paris to embark on her own career, and to have a good time. She was having a good time. Wasn't she?

Of course she was. Heavens, was it six o'clock already? Only just time to shower and change before she met her friends at the little bistro on the corner.

That October, when she had been at Brown and Lefèvre for almost three months, Lucy was invited to a drinks party by the head of her division at the bank.

The party was held in a very plush club, one Lucy hadn't been to before. Not part of my Paris at all, she thought, as she watched her gabardine coat being stowed away among the ranks of furs in the cloakroom.

The club was full of people she half recognised from work, most of them senior to herself, and their partners, most of whom she had never met before. She glanced around and caught sight of Herr Schliemann, her boss, looking exasperated, standing next to a thin woman in a turquoise dress. She headed across the room towards them.

The Schliemanns chatted politely for five minutes, then began to crane their heads past Lucy to follow the progress of a more important new arrival.

'Have you said hello to Madame Pasquier yet?' Herr Schliemann asked her.

That would be the division head's wife.

'I'm afraid I'm not sure...'

'Over there, in the red.' He nudged his head in the right direction.

'I'll go and introduce myself now. So nice to have met you, Frau Schliemann.'

Madame Pasquier was more charming, but she and her husband were busily greeting all their guests, and Lucy rapidly realised that she would merit no more than five minutes of their time, either. She was just glancing round again, hoping to locate a friend she could join and actually talk to, when Madame Pasquier said, 'Ah, Laurent. Do let me introduce you to Miss...'

'Lucy Sanderson,' Lucy said automatically, before her mind registered the fact that it really was Laurent. She had a split-second in which to steel herself, before her polite turn in his direction was complete, and she found her eyes connecting with his.

The look in them was so disconcerting that she hurriedly lowered her face.

'Lucy,' Laurent said, in a strange, wondering voice.

Lucy took a deep breath. 'How nice to see you,' she said brightly, not quite looking at Laurent. 'We're old acquaintances, Madame Pasquier, but it's a long time since we met.'

'Lucy,' Laurent repeated.

'Do excuse me,' said Madame Pasquier, mercifully disappearing to talk to somebody else.

The rest of the room seemed to fade away too, until there were just her and Laurent, together.

It was a Paris Laurent, of course, in a very dark suit, white shirt and bank tie, his hair unruffled, his tan no more than a faint memory. And it was a Paris Lucy facing him, she reminded herself. She wasn't any more the girl in the dripping T-shirt whom he had dived into Mahon harbour to rescue. Now she was a young executive in her party outfit, complete from pearl necklace to navy-blue pumps. Minorca was just as far behind her as it was behind him.

So why was he looking at her like this, with astonishment and wonder in his face? Why did the lightest touch of his hand against hers make her knees quiver and her insides turn to jelly? Why did it feel as if the long, empty months since she had last seen him had been wiped away, and it was only moments since she had last been in his arms?

She had never before felt so intensely female, so acutely conscious of the body hidden beneath her discreet blue sheath.

'Let's get out of here.' His hand tightened round hers, and he almost pulled her towards the door. Guests were still arriving at the party. Laurent guided her through them, polite but determined, nodding and murmuring to acquaintances as if to imply he would be back to talk to them later.

He waited while she retrieved her coat, and then somehow they reached the street. They came to a dead stop on the pavement.

Laurent looked around. 'There's a bar on the corner,' he said. 'Let's go there.'

They went to the bar, and he bought them each a brandy. They sat down, side by side on spindly metal chairs.

'It really is you,' Laurent said slowly.

'Really is.'

'I had no idea you were in Paris.'

Lucy hesitated. She didn't know what to say. This was Laurent, he looked and felt and sounded like Laurent. The very sight of him could still turn her world upside-down, but at the same time he was a stranger to her, and she to him. She knew scarcely anything about his life in Paris, and he hadn't even known that she was living in the same city.

'I've been here since July. I graduated this summer, and then I started working here.'

'You said that was what you wanted, to work in Paris.'

So he had remembered that. 'Did I?' Lucy said helplessly.

'You're on your own?'

'Yes.' There was a long pause before she plucked up courage to add, 'How about you?'

'Oh, I'm still alone.' He said it offhandedly, as if it was unthinkable that he might not be. He fell silent for a minute, cradling his brandy, then he said abruptly, 'Do you want to try again?'

Did she? For a moment, incredibly, it was as if she wasn't sure of her answer. The memory of that summer in Minorca was so intense that she felt she could almost smell the salt water of the harbour, feel the sun on her body and the wind from the *San Felipe* whipping through her hair. But this wasn't Minorca any more, and there was a year of hard work and loneliness separating this Lucy from that Lucy.

She looked at him, sideways, almost surreptitiously. He wasn't looking at her. He was nervous, she thought suddenly, a little afraid of the answer she might give. She could see the lines etched just a little deeper around his eyes and mouth. There were a few strands of silver amid the dark hair at his temples. 'Oh, I'm still alone,' he had said. She remembered Martine's comments about the once easy-going boss who now flew off the handle at the slightest excuse. And she suddenly felt absolutely sure that he needed her, even more than she needed him.

'I reckon so,' she said, in a quiet, steady voice.

He turned then, and met her eyes.

'I know there will be problems,' he said. 'There always are, in any relationship. But together, I think we will be able to handle them.'

'I think we will.'

Take it slowly, Lucy kept trying to tell herself. Take it slowly this time. There's no deadline, no end of the holiday to fear any more. But it was as if their meeting had lit a short fuse in both herself and Laurent. They could neither of them bear to wait any longer, and before long they were hailing a taxi and making their way back to his house.

The taxi dropped them in a quiet street in a part of the city that was completely unfamiliar to Lucy. It was the sort of street she would have expected him to live in, and yet it bore no resemblance to anything in her imaginings of his life in Paris. She had always envisaged him living in an apartment in a sleek modern block, a sort of city equivalent of his Minorcan villa, but instead this was an old house, tall and narrow, with steps leading up to the door.

Laurent fumbled for his key, then they were in a hallway, also narrow, and she was in his arms again.

They didn't even reach his bedroom. Just a living-room, one floor up, with a polished wood floor and a low leather sofa on to which they fell together. Lucy kicked off her pumps, and Laurent tore off her tights, and then he was in her, and she was wrapping her legs around his back, and crying out with a delight so fierce that the excitement and its release seemed to mingle in a blind intensity of feeling.

* * *

'At Brown and Lefèvre!' he exclaimed. 'You're working at Brown and Lefèvre?'

Lucy might have blushed, she thought, if she hadn't already been so flushed from his lovemaking. They were in his bath together, Lucy half on top of him in the deep squat tub, and a crazy mass of bubbles surrounding them and crowding over the brim.

'I wasn't chasing you,' she assured him. 'Honestly. It was the best job offer I got. I reckoned I couldn't possibly afford to turn it down.'

Laurent didn't listen. 'But you've been there how long?' he persisted.

'Three months now,' Lucy confessed.

'And I haven't seen you? You didn't pick up the phone and ring me? You didn't even tell me you were in Paris!'

He sounded so incredulous that it hardly seemed believable to Lucy that she could have thought it a sensible thing to do. But she had, she reminded herself. She'd mulled over it for hours, and convinced herself that she couldn't possibly do otherwise.

'I . . . oh, Laurent, it mattered so much!'

'Of course it mattered!' he exclaimed, jumping up so suddenly that he sent a great gush of water splashing on to the bathroom floor. 'Heavens, girl, do you know how much time I spent looking for you, after I left Minorca? I just couldn't believe my own idiocy in not asking for your address or your telephone number. I was convinced you couldn't be in Paris, but all the same I used to keep imagining I saw you. On the Metro, in bars, in the street: every time

I glimpsed a girl with long blonde hair I'd have to fight the temptation to chase after her.'

Lucy giggled. 'I haven't worn my hair loose since I got to Paris.'

'You should. Not at the bank, maybe, but outside it. Just for me.'

He reached for her hair as he spoke. It was still pinned, more or less, into its neat pleat. He pulled out a pin, and another.

'Laurent, it'll get wet,' Lucy protested, half jokingly trying to push his hands away.

'Let it. You can dry it later.' He ran his hands through her hair as it tumbled haphazardly on to his shoulders, and then pulled her hungrily to him for another kiss.

An alarm bell woke Lucy. An unfamiliar alarm, its electronic buzz unfairly insistent. She rolled over, sleepily, and connected with a solid, naked body.

Laurent. Laurent's bed, Laurent sleeping next to her. Laurent's wretched alarm, waking her up. And at what time? She squinted to see across the room to the luminous numerals. Six o'clock!

Laurent stirred, and flung out an arm that landed across her. His eyes slowly opened.

'Morning,' he murmured. He flung back the covers and got out of bed.

'You can't get up at six o'clock,' Lucy protested sleepily. 'Not the morning after a party.'

'Not to mention a night like last night,' Laurent teased. He was wide awake now, unfairly alert. 'Oh, yes, I can. And so can you. Unless you were thinking of going to work in your party dress . . .'

'Heavens!' Lucy sat up. 'I suppose you're right.'

By the time she had showered and put back on— temporarily—the clothes she had worn the night before, Laurent was already in the kitchen, the table was half-set for breakfast, and a delicious smell of fresh coffee was wafting through the house.

'I do have a housekeeper,' he explained, 'but she doesn't come in until eight. Croissants?'

'Please. One croissant.'

'Help yourself. And you like your coffee white, with no sugar. See, I remembered?' Laurent grinned, and pushed a large cupful across to her.

'You remembered everything,' she murmured, as she spread a shockingly thick layer of apricot jam across the crispy skin of her croissant.

'Every last thing. Though I have a whole lot more to learn about you now, I can see.'

'And I about you.'

She watched him as he sat down and began to tear his own croissant apart. How true, she thought: they had a long way still to travel. She had never even seen him in the mornings before. It was all new to her, this mixture of sudden alertness combined with a rumpled vulnerability. His house was strange to her, his friends would be strangers, his son Gilles—she didn't even know what make of car he drove in Paris.

'What are you thinking?' he asked suddenly.

Lucy grinned. 'How odd it is, that I should know you so little, and yet love you so much.'

'That's chemistry,' Laurent teased, raising his coffee-cup to her. 'It's true for me, too. I never even stopped to imagine, on Minorca, what you would be like in your real life, when you were back in England, what kind of things you would do, what clothes you would wear, how you would do your hair. I told myself right from the start that you and I were two people from different worlds, and that any proper relationship between us was unimaginable. But every time I saw you I wanted you more. At first I thought I didn't want even a friendship, and then I thought, all right, I want to see her again, but I won't let it get serious. And *then* I thought all right, I want to make love to her, but it can't be more than a brief holiday romance...'

'And then you went.'

'And then I thought, good heavens, I can't bear to lose her, and yet when we were together I never even told her how much I loved her!'

'You never did,' Lucy agreed, with a touch of sadness.

'What a blind fool I was! I'd been so wrapped up in the misery of my divorce that I didn't even realise I was getting over it. And even then, perhaps I wasn't really ready for a new commitment. But I'm ready now, I promise you.'

'So am I,' Lucy whispered.

'We can't make it all happen overnight. We still need to learn so much about each other. And there is Gilles to think of, too. It will take time for him to get to know you, and to get accustomed to the idea of having a stepmother. But I'm sure now, and I think you are too, that we will be able to solve all the problems that come up, and that we'll be together eventually.' He gave a slow smile. 'Perhaps we can turn our holiday in Minorca next summer into our honeymoon.'

'Darling,' Lucy said, 'there's nowhere in the world I'd rather go.'

'Nor I.' Laurent glanced at his watch. 'But right now,' he exclaimed, 'we have to get to work!' He stood up abruptly, and grabbed his jacket from the back of his chair. 'Are you ready to go?'

'Yes,' said Lucy. 'I'm ready.'

CHAPTER ELEVEN

IT WAS a hot August day when Laurent and Lucy Buckley and Gilles landed at Mahon airport. Alonzo was waiting at the arrivals desk to greet them. He smiled so broadly that Lucy instantly decided she was going to forget the past, and start to like him. She and Laurent piled their cases into the car, and let Gilles sit in the front seat as Alonzo drove them along the familiar roads from the airport, through Mahon town, and along the road that led down the side of Mahon harbour, past Nelson's Golden Farm, and to their villa.

As soon as the cases were unloaded into the hall, and Juana had been greeted, Alonzo and Juana tactfully disappeared. Gilles, bursting with excitement, paused only a moment longer before rushing off down the steps to the harbour, with a warning to be careful echoing behind him. Laurent dashed to the phone to make an urgent call to the bank. And Lucy took only a cursory look at the pile of suitcases that needed unpacking, then wandered instead into the courtyard.

A yellow sun blazed down from a cloudless sky, striking right through the cool water in the swimming pool. It looked an unreal blue. Lucy pulled off her sandal, and dipped in a toe. It was just as freezing as she remembered it.

It was two years since she had been to the villa, but it was all almost exactly as she remembered it. Alonzo had repainted the walls with the same white paint. She could see through the open doors to the living-room, where Laurent, his back turned on the sun, was gesticulating on the phone. There were the doors to his bedroom—their bedroom, now—where he had carried her on that memorable night two years before. There were the table and chairs where the two of them had sat on that first day and lunched together, with Lucy in her damp bikini. She even traced the path round to Juana's yard, where the herbs in their pots seemed to have grown higher and bushier.

The villa held such special memories for her. Not all of them were happy, but the sad ones had been dulled by time, and the good ones had grown even brighter, now she knew how happily their story had ended.

She walked to the head of the harbour steps, and looked down over the wooden railing. Gilles was running up and down the quay. He paused by the steps in the centre, and, stretching out at full length on the sunwarmed wood, reached to dip his hand in the green water. Then he jumped up, shaking it dry, and ran to investigate the boathouse.

Lucy left him to it. This was his exploration, his time to remember; he had stayed at the villa before, with his mother. She retraced her steps and went back inside.

A great bunch of roses in full bloom, pink and white and red, sat on the kitchen table, in a pretty blue and

yellow bowl that she didn't recognise. A note was
propped up by the side.

'Welcome home.'

It was in Sophie's round, scrawly handwriting. Lucy
was still looking at it when Laurent came into the
room. He moved to her side, slipping his arm round
her and bending down to read it.

'Funny,' he said. 'That's exactly what I was going
to say myself.'

Harlequin Presents

Coming Next Month

1231 THAT SPECIAL TOUCH Anne Beaumont
Elisa enjoys her summer sketching tourists in Corfu, which makes a good
refuge from her problems back home. Now it seems that Rafe Sinclair and his
daughter, Penny, are about to present her with equally challenging ones here.

1232 THE FALCON'S MISTRESS Emma Darcy
Bethany runs afoul of autocratic Prince Zakr, ruler of Bayrar, almost as soon as
her plane lands. He thinks he can bend her to his will as easily as he trains his
hunting falcons. But Bethany has plans of her own....

1233 LOVE'S REWARD Robyn Donald
Jake Ferrars has an overwhelming impact on women, as Cathy Durrant has on
men. Two beautiful people, each one knowing about the other. But how can
they possibly believe that the rumors they've heard about each other
are true?

1234 AWAKENING DREAMS Vanessa Grant
They are lucky to be alive—but trekking out of the wilderness with Jesse
Campbell is not Crystal's idea of normal travel, especially for a city tax auditor.
But a quick assessment of their situation shows they have no alternative.

1235 TODAY, TOMORROW AND FOREVER Sally Heywood
Inheriting part ownership of a Mediterranean island is such a thrill that Shanna
wants to see it right away. Meeting Paul Elliott on the way is a bonus, until
Shanna realizes that he's keeping a secret from her.

1236 SEDUCTIVE STRANGER Charlotte Lamb
Returning to England after ten years, Prue wants to see her father again and to
find out the truth about the past. She doesn't welcome interference from
Josh Killane—he makes her temper soar and her heart beat faster!

1237 STRANGE ENCOUNTER Sally Wentworth
Kelly Baxter, after her parents' death, tracks down lost relatives in England.
She can't help wondering, though, when she does discover a long-lost cousin in
the Cotswolds, why Byron Thorne is most reluctant to let them meet.

1238 TEMPORARY BRIDE Patricia Wilson
Charlotte can't let her beloved uncle go to prison, even if he did commit fraud.
Kit Landor says he won't prosecute if she will marry him. With no other
alternative, Charlotte agrees—but doesn't intend to let him have it all his
own way....

Available in January wherever paperback books are sold, or through
Harlequin Reader Service:

In the U.S.
901 Fuhrmann Blvd.
P.O. Box 1397
Buffalo, N.Y. 14240-1397

In Canada
P.O. Box 603
Fort Erie, Ontario
L2A 5X3

CHRISTMAS IS FOR KIDS

Spend this holiday season with nine very special children. Children whose wishes come true at the magical time of Christmas.

Read American Romance's CHRISTMAS IS FOR KIDS— heartwarming holiday stories in which children bring together four couples who fall in love. Meet:

Frank, Dorcas, Kathy, Candy and Nicky—They become friends at St. Christopher's orphanage, but they really want to be adopted and become part of a real family, in #321 *A Carol Christmas* by Muriel Jensen.

Patty—She's a ten-year-old certified genius, but she wants what every little girl wishes for: a daddy of her own, in #322 *Mrs. Scrooge* by Barbara Bretton.

Amy and Flash—Their mom is about to deliver their newest sibling any day, but Christmas just isn't the same now—not without their dad. More than anything they want their family reunited for Christmas, in #323 *Dear Santa* by Margaret St. George.

Spencer—Living with his dad and grandpa in an all-male household has its advantages, but Spence wants Santa to bring him a mommy to love, in #324 *The Best Gift of All* by Andrea Davidson.

These children will win your hearts as they entice—and matchmake—the adults into a true romance. This holiday, invite them—and the four couples they bring together—into your home.

Look for all four CHRISTMAS IS FOR KIDS books available now from Harlequin American Romance. And happy holidays!

XMAS-KIDS-1R

Especially for you,
Christmas from
HARLEQUIN HISTORICALS

An enchanting collection of three Christmas
stories by some of your favorite authors captures
the spirit of the season in the 1800s

TUMBLEWEED CHRISTMAS by Kristin James

A "Bah, humbug" Texas rancher meets his match in his
new housekeeper, a woman determined to bring the spirit
of a Tumbleweed Christmas into his life—and love into
his heart.

A CINDERELLA CHRISTMAS by Lucy Elliot

The perfect granddaughter, sister and aunt, Mary Hillyer
seemed destined for spinsterhood until Jack Gates arrived
to discover a woman with dreams and passions that were
meant to be shared during a Cinderella Christmas.

HOME FOR CHRISTMAS
by Heather Graham Pozzessere

The magic of the season brings peace Home For
Christmas when a Yankee captain and a Southern heiress
fall in love during the Civil War.

Look for HARLEQUIN HISTORICALS CHRISTMAS
STORIES wherever Harlequin books are sold.

Wonderful, luxurious gifts can be yours with proofs-of-purchase from any specially marked "Indulge A Little" Harlequin or Silhouette book with the Offer Certificate properly completed, plus a check or money order (do not send cash) to cover postage and handling payable to Harlequin/Silhouette "Indulge A Little, Give A Lot" Offer. We will send you the specified gift.

Mail-in-Offer

OFFER CERTIFICATE

Item:	A. Collector's Doll	B. Soaps in a Basket	C. Potpourri Sachet	D. Scented Hangers
# of Proofs-of -Purchase	18	12	6	4
Postage & Handling	$3.25	$2.75	$2.25	$2.00
Check One				

Name _____

Address _____ Apt. # _____

City _____ State _____ Zip _____

ONE PROOF OF PURCHASE

To collect your free gift by mail you must include the necessary number of proofs-of-purchase plus postage and handling with offer certificate.

HP-3

Harlequin®/Silhouette®

Mail this certificate, designated number of proofs-of-purchase and check or money order for postage and handling to:

INDULGE A LITTLE
P.O. Box 9055
Buffalo, N.Y. 14269-9055